West Tennessee Taproot

A Collection of Short Stories Poetry & Songs

by Myrlen Britt

2nd Edition

Published by Main Street Publishing
d n english Publisher
P.O. Box 696 Jackson Tennessee 38302
Phone: 731-427-7379

MSP e-mail - words@mspbooks.com

Mr. Britt's e-mail: myrlenbritt@aol.com

<u>Credits</u>
Written by Myrlen Britt

Cover Photo by Renee Britt
Charlene Johnson © Grandchildren's Photo - Page 113

Cover Art, Layout and Editing
Annette W. Galloway

Assistant Editor
Michael F. Duke

Printed and bound in New York
by NetPub Corporation

ISBN - 0-9710470-6-5

DEDICATION

This little book is dedicated to my grandchildren, Josh Logan, Morgan and Kaitlyn Britt, and any future grandchildren I might be blessed with.

My life long desire has been to be a writer. I finally accepted the fact that I was not destined to write "The Great American Novel". However, with encouragement from d n english, Annette Galloway, and my family, I decided to write about things that interested me.

The following pages contain short stories, prose, several essays and even a hymn. I hope that someday, long after I've crossed over Jordan, my grandchildren will read this booklet and learn some things that made their PawPaw tick.

October 15, 2001

Myrlen Britt

Table of Contents

WEST TENNESSEE TAPROOT

My roots run deep in the West Tennessee soil, over one hundred and fifty years deep.

My great-great grandfather, Beacum Britt, first came to West Tennessee in the 1830s with his first wife, Dallie Wallace Britt, and at least some of their seven children. According to family lore there was a second earthquake in the area and they, along with other families, returned to North Carolina. Here, Dallie died, and, as was the custom in those days, Beacum married her sister, Deborah, twenty-seven years his junior.

They had eleven children together, and sometime during the marriage they returned to West Tennessee in a covered wagon drawn by two oxen. He was for a time a prosperous farmer. He was living in McNairy County, Tennessee, in 1860 and my great-grandfather, Hans, is listed in the census as being seven years old.

We always called him 'Uncle Hans" instead of Grandpa. I think our mother gave him that title. He used to visit us when I was a small child and he was in his late eighties. He told a story of his dad taking him to the battlefield at Shiloh shortly after the terrible battle there. He said the Confederate soldiers were piled in a trench and some of their feet were sticking through the thin layer of dirt. Other curiosity seekers obviously were there. He said a man pulled on one of the boots and it came off in his hand with the foot still inside. He lost no time in throwing it as far from him as he could.

My great-grandfather, "Uncle Hans" Britt

As the twenty-first century gets under way we Americans have become creatures of the present. Those who know about these things tell us that we move on average every five years. There seems to be no stability in our lives anymore. My unprofessional opinion is that this is a major cause of the breakup of our families. It has to be some fundamental change in our culture that causes one out of every two marriages to end in divorce. Mom working outside the home doesn't help matters either.

In the years following World War II we saw our families migrating north in search of jobs. The Sunshine Belt now beckons our wayward natives to return home. But we are also experiencing an influx of other folks to our sunny climate and old fashioned mores. For better or worse it is happening.

As I get older I am reminded more and more of the values we took for granted in rural West Tennessee half a century ago.

I like to remember the stories my great grandfather told about the Civil War and even earlier. Somehow it connects me with the past. I like the feeling that I actually remember someone who was alive before the Civil War was fought.

During my childhood in the late thirties and through the forties it was not unusual for our small house to contain, in addition to our substantial family, some other relative who had no place to go. This was repeated in probably a majority of farm families. Today, the counterparts of these folks are living on the streets of our cities and underneath bridges.

I have lived in three states and several cities over the past forty years, a necessary evil in my chosen career of retail management. However, my heart has always remained anchored to the soil in West Tennessee. With the passing of time the anchor only holds more securely.

AN AUTUMN MEMORY

Outside, the late November clouds hung low and dark over the rolling hills. The trees behind the barn were bare except for a few brown leaves that clung to the branches as if trying to hold off the impending winter. Overhead, a flock of Canada geese honked, as they winged their way to a more favorable climate.

The homemade ladder, nailed to the wall of the cattle stall, reached upward into the black hole that was the entrance to the hayloft. The stables below gave off a pungent, almost acrid, smell of decayed manure from many years past,

In the loft the faint aroma of alfalfa remained after more than a decade. A cold drizzle began to fall, caressing the tin roof with an almost inaudible sound. From a dark corner came the soft coo of a pigeon as he assured his mate there was no danger. In the distance a dog barked as he chased after his master in the rain. Age-old peanut shells mixed with pecan hulls littered the floor. The damp chill of the late afternoon evoked bittersweet memories that had lain dormant for years.

Two hours earlier I had left Nashville for the one hundred mile drive to my boyhood home and had been propelled almost a half century into the past. The gray, weather beaten barn seemed smaller than I remembered, but as I climbed the ladder to the loft, I was overcome by the memories. As the drizzle became a torrent of rain drumming on the roof like so many hoof beats of a runaway herd, I closed my eyes and could almost hear my dad's voice.

It was four o'clock. Soon it would be time to milk Rosie and help my brothers feed the other animals. At six Momma would call us to supper. Freshly churned buttermilk and hot cornbread. Maybe tonight fried chicken as well. There would be bread pudding for dessert, a staple in the rural south in the forties, inexpensive, but served with an abundance of love.

After the supper dishes were washed out came the books, and homework was finished by the flickering light of a kerosene lamp. Then a bath by the open fireplace and finally to bed.

The warm southern air suddenly collided with the cold front and with a loud boom of thunder I was yanked back to reality. The rain was still coming down in sheets as it blew through the cracks of the barn wall. It was late and my wife was expecting me home by bedtime.

As I made my way through the muddy barnyard to my car I realized the dampness on my cheeks hadn't come from the rain. Thomas Wolfe said, "You can never go home again." Perhaps not, but on a chilly, damp November afternoon I came as close as anyone ever has.

A TRUE GHOST STORY

I remember two very distinct things about my Dad. He was known to be willing to "give you the shirt off his back," which was sometimes almost all he possessed, and he did not believe in ghosts. Nonetheless, he told this story many times when I was a boy. When pressed for an explanation he would stare off in the distance, shake his head, and reply, "I don't know what the answer is."

My Dad was fourteen years old in 1913, and his brother was two or three years younger. As was the practice in rural communities then, the local people would put their mailboxes on a wagon wheel or some other structure on the main road. This way the mail carrier would not have to travel the side roads to deliver to individual houses. This was necessary since many times the side roads were virtually impassable after a rain. My grandparents and their neighbors put their boxes at the local school building.

My grandmother needed something from the mailman, perhaps stamps, and sent my dad and Uncle Jesse to meet the mailman. This was during one of the periods that school was dismissed to allow the children to work in the fields.

Dad and his teacher were close and had always shared the shade of the big oak tree in front of the school building to eat lunch. Sadly, his teacher had died the past year. Therein lies our ghost story.

My Dad sat down under the oak tree to wait for the mailman when the door to the school building opened and someone came out. As he walked toward my dad and uncle they realized it was Mr. Virgil Corbett, the deceased teacher. He came up and said, "How have you been, Wiley?" My uncle was so frightened he almost wet his pants, but my Dad made conversation with the "ghost."

Mr. Corbett had a brother, Vincent, who had moved to Arkansas, and he asked if anyone had heard from him. After some further conversation he said, "Well, Wiley, it was good to see you again, but I must go now." He walked past the school building and came to the wood's edge overlooking a steep bluff, and there he simply disappeared.

My Dad died in 1979 at age eighty. I asked him before he died to repeat the story and he did. I don't remember all the things they talked about, but he and my uncle, who was a Baptist minister, declared the story was true. I asked him again, as I had when I was small, what he thought had happened, since I knew how strongly he refused to believe in ghosts, but I got the same, strange look as he stared off in space and replied, "I don't know, son. I just don't know.

AN OLD YELLOW BUS

The old yellow bus coughs and sputters to life reluctantly as the volunteer driver coaxes it ever so gently. She has transported hundreds of children to school who were now adults and she still has some life in her.

It's late August and it's hot. The asphalt streets in the housing projects are so hot they have liquefied in some places. We are here to gather the children and take them to local churches to study the Bible.

The old bus has "Inner City Ministry" proudly stenciled on her side. She is one of dozens that have fanned out over the city on this sweltering Thursday night.

Our group is composed of nine to thirteen-year olds, both boys and girls. As we move slowly along the narrow, winding streets there are clusters of young people standing on the sidewalks with nothing to do. Cadillacs and Mercedes parked along the curbs are not uncommon. They belong to the pimps and pushers. You can see them fearlessly plying their trade in the open without any concern for the young lives that they ruin.

We turn a corner and the blue lights of a patrol car catch our eyes. Two officers are talking to several scantily clad women, prostitutes, no doubt, and some are the mothers of the children we'll be picking up. We're a cheap source of baby-sitting for some.

We turn another corner and see a crowd gathered around a Dumpster. Someone has started a fire in it, and the excitement breaks the monotony for the teens with a sprinkling of adults mixed in.

I'm a bus captain, and my job is to keep the peace and prevent any injuries to the children or the driver.

Tonight we have a young minister riding with us. A suburban church pays his salary so he can devote all his time to working with the parents in the projects, encouraging them to allow their children to spend one night a week during the school year studying the Bible.

We move slowly along the narrow streets, stopping here and there to pick up a group of youngsters. Our rules are strict: girls are seated on one side of the bus and boys on the other. Tonight we are filled to capacity; everybody wants to go, because the church building is air-conditioned.

We move out of the projects and head for the interstate, and the problems begin. A twelve-year old in an adult size body decides it's too hot with the windows cracked. He opens a window wide enough to get his upper torso outside the bus. Someone tells me, and I try to get him back inside before a flying rock or other debris causes him injury. I put my hands on his shoulder and tug. He sits down abruptly and snarls, "Keep your hands off me man, you can't touch me." I put on my best drill sergeant voice and demeanor and win the battle, at least for now. He sits but clearly is not happy about it.

Some of the other boys begin to rag him for complying with my orders. I finally get them under control and we continue on our half-hour drive to the church building.

I'm tired. I've been doing this for two years and I'm suffering burnout. I say to the young minister, "Brother, this is my last night. I'm just too old for all this. I don't feel like I'm making any progress." He isn't happy about my decision, but he assures me he understands.

We reach the building and begin to unload our precious cargo. The girls for the most part are co-operative and head into the building. The boy in the window comes off and at once attacks one of the boys who laughed at him. "Fight, fight!" rings out as the others take sides and yell encouragement to their favorites.

I dive in and manage to separate them. The driver helps me herd them into the building. They immediately go in several directions, some to the water fountain, some to the men's room, some trying to hide and slip back outside.

Through some miracle we manage to get them to the correct rooms, then find we're short of teachers. So now I'm a teacher with no lesson plan. I've drawn a roomful of twelve and thirteen-year olds. I read a story from the Bible and try to get them involved. One or two participate, but the others have no interest.

I have fifteen minutes to go and I'm out of material. Deciding to take a poll, I ask each boy what he wants to be when he grows up. All but one wants to play professional sports and get rich and leave the projects. Only one said he would like to become a medical doctor.

I tell them about Justice Clarence Thomas and others who overcame their environment to become successful. They're quiet for the first time all evening. The classes finally end and we load the old yellow bus to take them home to the projects.

They're rowdy and almost out of control. We enter the projects and pass by the Dumpster. The fire is still smoldering, but there's not enough flame to keep its audience. Most of the pimps and dealers have left for the night, leaving their poison behind as they go away with their pockets stuffed with their ill-gotten gains.

We stop for the last group to disembark. I'm surer than ever before that I'll not be back next week. The boys leave the bus first, then the girls line up to get off. A pretty little girl with beautiful, liquid brown eyes, wearing a new dress from the dollar store, stops where I'm sitting. She seems nervous, and then she puts her arms around me and says, "I love you. Thank-you for loving us." She kisses me lightly on the cheek. Then clutching her Bible and the lesson she's studied tonight, she's quickly caught up in the throng of the crowd and she's gone.

I have a lump in my throat and tears in my eyes as we head for the garage. When I get off I walk over to the young minister and tell him, "I'll see you next week." We embrace.

As I leave the parking area and head across town to my comfortable suburban home, I see there is a full moon, and the stars are like diamonds suspended from black crepe.

I remember Jesus' words: "Unless you become as one of these little ones, you cannot enter the kingdom of heaven." Half an hour later I pull into my driveway. I sit there for a long time. I thank God for the opportunities we have to show His love to those who might never feel loved, and I thank him for the little girl and for an old yellow bus.

Natchez Trace Pecan Tree
Believed to have been planted by soldier in "Old Hickory's" Unit.

THE PECAN TREE

CHAPTER ONE

Jeremy Tarwater stood nervously behind the hastily built ramparts, waiting for the impending attack by the British. "Are you loaded, Tarwater?" A gruff old veteran asked.

"Yes sir," said Jeremy through clenched teeth.

"Keep your chin up, boy, and your powder dry."

Major General Andrew Jackson, "Old Hickory", had quickly brought together his motley crew of four thousand men to defend New Orleans against a British force of more than twenty thousand redcoats.

The British commander, General Parkenham, had thousands of seasoned troops, as well as new recruits, under his command.

Jeremy was sixteen years old, dressed in the tattered uniform of a Tennessee Militiaman. He had a sick feeling in his stomach as he looked to the right and left and saw veteran soldiers, as well as "free men of color," former Haitian slaves. Further down, the famous pirate, Jean LaFitte, and his swaggering band of outlaws protected the ramparts.

He thought of home in Tennessee, his pa and momma who begged him not to join Jackson's troops as they paraded down the streets of Nashville.

He no longer felt the same defiance to his pa that he did months before when he packed a little food and sneaked out of the log cabin he had helped Pa build. "I sure wish I'd listened to Pa," he thought.

Suddenly, the British started the attack. The battlefield in front of Jeremy became a sea of red as the soldiers of the Crown attacked across the open field, testifying to the utter stupidity of military leaders that still is prevalent today.

The order was given. " Fire!" Muskets on either side of Jeremy begin to fire. He was so scared he could hardly lift the old squirrel rifle to his shoulder. He didn't want to kill anyone. Right then, he wanted to go home. Even twelve-hour days helping Pa on the farm looked good to him now. The second order of, "Fire!" broke his train of thought, and he aimed at a red uniform racing toward him across an open field. His target was a young lieutenant, waving his saber and urging his men forward. Though they fell like flies around him, still he came forward.

Jeremy squeezed the trigger and the bullet found its mark squarely between the eyes of the young officer.

He fell forward and his saber fell harmlessly by his side. Jeremy was so sick he wanted to vomit, but he knew he couldn't allow that to happen. His friend from Tennessee, Johnny Beauchamp, turned and slapped him on the back. "You got yourself an office..." His voice never completed the sentence, as a British bullet struck him in the throat and killed him instantly. He fell into Jeremy's arms and his blood covered his friend's shirt.

Soldiers don't cry, he quickly learned as the battle waned and soon the firing stopped. A cheer went up along the ramparts. It was a resounding victory for Old Hickory and his ragtag army. The British suffered more than two thousand killed and wounded, while the Americans lost only six killed and ten wounded. Months later they would learn that a treaty had already been signed two weeks before the battle occurred.

By the end of January the troops prepared to pull out of Louisiana and go home to Tennessee. Old Hickory led the main body himself, north through Mississippi, then along the Natchez Trace to Nashville. At Tupelo he directed Colonel John Coffee to take his Tennessee Militia directly north into West Tennessee to monitor the activities of the Creek and Chickasaw Indians.

The red clay of north Mississippi clung to Jeremy's boots and made walking a torture. It rained for days, and as the small band reached the Tennessee line the rain turned to snow. Jeremy missed his friend, Johnny, but the constant backslapping of his comrades who had decided he was a hero buoyed his spirits. "Jeremy killed himself an officer," they boasted, seeming somehow to share in the glory by saying it out loud and often. No doubt, by the time they got home they would each relate to their friends and family how they had killed a British officer.

The north branch of the Trace took the group through the heavily forested area that would become Henderson

County, Tennessee. Their rations were low and they foraged for food, occasionally killing a bear or deer. Jeremy had left New Orleans with his knapsack and pockets filled with a strange, new nut that had a very good flavor, something akin to the hickory nuts he was used to eating in middle Tennessee. The Creole people called them "pecans," and he wanted to save some for his momma, but with the scarcity of food he had gradually eaten all but one nut. He put it in his trouser pocket, determined to save it.

After many weeks of fighting the mud, snow and cold they decided to camp for a few days before crossing the Tennessee River. That night some of Jeremy's comrades decided to celebrate. A few had some cheap whisky they had bought in New Orleans, and since they would be home soon this would be a good night to chase away the cold. Colonel Coffee gave them permission to enjoy a nip with the roasted deer they had killed that afternoon.

As the night wore on a few had more than a nip and soon persuaded Jeremy to join them. His pa had always preached, "It's not wise for a man to allow demon rum to rule his life. A man does foolish things when he drinks." After two drinks he felt better than he had since Johnny had died, so he had another. Soon the liquor was gone and one by one the soldiers had retired to their tents and fell into a drunken sleep.

Jeremy stumbled toward his tent and ran head-on into his sergeant. "Tarwater, what's wrong with you, boy? Are you drunk, soldier?" he barked.

"Just celebrating, Sergeant," he mumbled.

"We're in hostile territory, Tarwater. We could be attacked any minute by those renegade Creeks. A lot of help you'd be, boy, in your state!" he thundered. "I just inspected your tent, and there are biscuit crumbs all over the place. Clean it up before you go to sleep," he ordered.

Buoyed by the false courage found in the whisky bottle, Jeremy talked back. "I'm a hero. Why should I pick up crumbs? The officers never do."

"What did you say, soldier?" The non-com's face flushed at this obvious disregard of his order.

Still feeling cocky, Jeremy said, "I ain't gonna pick up no crumbs!"

The sergeant grabbed his shirtfront and shook him angrily. "Are you disobeying my order, Tarwater?"

A slight sense of fear pushed through Jeremy's alcohol saturated brain only to be pushed aside by the false sense of courage. "I said, I warn't gonna pick up crumbs," he stubbornly insisted.

"You leave me no choice, boy. Let's go see the colonel."

Lieutenant Overton, Colonel Coffee's aide, emerged from his tent rubbing the sleep from his eyes. "What's the meaning of this, Sergeant Bowen? Don't you know what time it is?" he barked.

"I'm sorry, sir, but I need to see the colonel," the sergeant insisted. He and Colonel Coffee went way back together, when they both fought the Creek Indians. The colonel respected him and the sergeant knew that Lieutenant Overton wouldn't dare try to stop him from seeing the commander.

"Very well, wait here. I'll wake him, but be prepared for a royal chewing. You know he likes his sleep."

It seemed like an hour before the colonel appeared before his tent, pulling his suspenders up as he came forward.

"Well, Sergeant Bowen, what's so all-fired important that it couldn't wait till morning?" he groused.

"I'm sorry to wake you, Colonel, but Private Tarwater here has a little problem that needs your attention, sir." said Bowen.

"Private, are you drunk?" roared the colonel.

Jeremy's brain was still foggy with the alcohol. He tried to reply but his tongue felt so thick he could only stammer, "Y-yes sir."

"Who's his company commander, Sergeant?" he demanded

"Captain Morgan, H Company, sir," Bowen replied.

"Lieutenant Overton, fetch Morgan, and bring Major Miles along, too." ordered Coffee.

"Private Tarwater, aren't you the soldier that killed a British officer?"

"Yes sir," he mumbled, now scared as he realized the gravity of his offense.

"You fought bravely in New Orleans, soldier, but that doesn't excuse you of your actions tonight. Our scouts just today observed some Creek activity not two days from here. We could come under attack at any time."

Jeremy was almost totally sober by the time the other officers arrived, still not fully dressed.

Acting under the rules of war, Coffee called the four officers and Bowen together, along with the corporal of the guard who was given the task of keeping an eye on the prisoner.

"Gentlemen, the rules of combat are clear. We have no choice but to find this soldier guilty of gross misconduct, insubordination to a non-commissioned officer, and drunk while on duty in hostile territory." the colonel intoned.

"If we were in garrison it would be different, but we're not. We all fought the Creeks in Mobile and Pensacola, and we all realize the importance of being ready for an attack on a moment's notice."

They all sensed where this was going and were uncomfortable with what they knew was coming.

"Sergeant, have the corporal of the guard bring the prisoner forward." The colonel himself looked unhappy.

"Private Jeremy Tarwater, I have heard from Sergeant Bowen and you. I've also observed for myself that you are drunk and incapable of defending our perimeter in case of attack. I have no choice other than to order that tomorrow at sunrise you be executed by firing squad!"

Jeremy reeled as the words sank into his brain. "Please, sir, I'm sorry. I don't want to die!" he begged. "I haven't seen my mother for 'most a year, sir," he begged.

"I'm sorry, soldier, but I have the safety of a thousand men to look out for. What you did tonight endangered all of us.

"Major Miles, have your first sergeant select three men from companies other than H, none above the rank of corporal. Have one musket packed with wadding and powder and no bullet, and let each man think he has that rifle," he ordered.

"Yes, sir."

"Corporal of the Guard, take charge of the prisoner and make sure he's fed before sun up. That's all, gentlemen." He turned and walked swiftly into his tent.

The colonel stood in the darkness of his tent for a long time. Finally he lit a candle and rummaged through his gear and retrieved a worn Bible. He sat at the small table in the center of the tent and opened the book to the twenty-third Psalm. He was still reading when the sun broke over the eastern horizon splashing pinks and purples on the thin clouds. His cheeks were wet with tears.

The entire regiment was summoned and the corporal

of the guard led Jeremy by the arm to a bluff overlooking a stand of hardwood trees that had just begun to leaf out in the early spring.

His hands were tied behind his back, and the rag that was put over his eyes covered his tearstained cheeks.

Colonel Coffee approached him and asked, "Do you have any last words, soldier?"

"I just want to see my momma once more before I die, sir," he pleaded.

Even Major Miles, hardened by a dozen battles, had a tear in his eye as Coffee turned to the corporal and said, "Carry on."

The birds, just waking for the day, had begun their songs, but as the three men stood at attention awaiting the order they all dreaded to hear, the singing stopped as though they knew something was about to happen.

"Squad, attention, ready arms, aim, fire!" Three shots broke the stillness and Jeremy slumped to the ground. Major Miles stepped forward and knelt by the boy's body, tears now streaming down his unshaven face. "He's dead," he announced.

The burial detail had dug a shallow grave on the bluff overlooking a freshwater spring, and now they lifted the body and laid it next to the opening in the earth. They removed the rags from his eyes and gently closed the lids, then they removed his boots; supplies were in short order and another soldier would benefit from his death.

Colonel Coffee stood over the thin body of the boy and quietly said, "May God have mercy on your soul and on all of us."

The attack they all feared never materialized and a week later the regiment moved out. They would build rafts when they reached the Tennessee River and would be home in time for spring planting.

The spring rains fell on the grave and the hot summer sun beamed down on it. As the clothing and the body decomposed the pecan in his pocket took root and grew. It wasn't long before the young tender shoot pushed its head through the rich West Tennessee soil. The deer came and ate the grass all around it but never ate the young plant.

The Chickasaw came to the spring and saw the crude cross that the soldiers had made from wood taken from the supply wagon and held together by rawhide.

In reality the regiment had never been in danger. There were no more than two dozen renegade Creek in West Tennessee and the Chickasaw had no desire to fight the white man.

The years passed and the Indians came to believe the place where Jeremy was buried was haunted. They told stories of seeing mysterious lights at night, and they said that in the early spring the sweet water from the hillside was so bitter that even the animals refused to drink it.

More than twenty years passed since Jeremy's untimely death, and white settlers were beginning to arrive from Virginia and North Carolina.

CHAPTER TWO

Nath and Deborah Beacum came over the Smokies in a covered wagon drawn by two oxen. They had two boys. Noah was fourteen and Benjamin was twelve. They staked a claim on a hundred acres overlooking a spring and lots of hardwood trees, perfect for building a cabin.

They arrived just as spring was coming into bloom. They slept in the wagon and Deborah cooked over an open fire while Nath and the boys turned the rich soil and planted corn, beans, squash and other vegetable seeds they had brought with them.

"Ma, we got us a good start here," Nath would say to Deborah almost every day.

Once the seeds had been planted in the open spaces they began the arduous task of clearing more land using the trees they cut to start building a rough cabin.

After a hard morning of labor the boys were doing some exploring of their new home and came upon the pecan tree. They had plenty of nut trees in North Carolina but had never seen a tree like this before. Its trunk was no more than ten inches in diameter and maybe twenty feet tall, but it was loaded with a strange nut with a green hull. They pulled a few off the tree and ran toward the unfinished cabin, yelling, "Pa! Pa, look what we found!" He, too, was unsure what they were. He cautioned them not to cut the tree down. They would wait for the fall to see what these strange nuts tasted like.

As spring turned to summer the long hours of daylight afforded the family plenty of time to clear several acres and build a large one-room cabin with a fireplace.

Noah and Ben continued to sleep in the wagon or on a quilt on the ground when the weather was nice, while their pa hewed boards by hand to add a lean-to onto the back of the house. This would become their bedroom when the weather turned cold.

Nath had been a successful peanut farmer in Wake County and he applied his skills to this new land. The soil was perfectly suited for peanuts and as the years passed he became quite prosperous. By the late forties the cabin had been replaced with a comfortable three bedroom home with a parlor and dining room. During these years the pecan tree grew and produced an abundance of nuts each year.

Deborah had learned to make delicious pies with the strange little nut. From time to time strange things happened in the vicinity of the tree, but Nath was not a superstitious man. He always had a logical answer to any question the boys brought to him. He was never able to convince the boys, or even Deborah that it was a natural occurrence that the animals never drank from the fresh water spring during the middle of March.

Many nights, while coon hunting, the dogs would refuse to go near the pecan tree and would stand stiff legged and growl and bare their teeth. The boys reported over the years that they had seen strange lights moving about underneath the tree.

Noah was thirty in the spring of 1853 when he married Nancy Parish, whose folks had the farm next to theirs. When the peanuts were harvested in the fall he could hardly wait for the birth of his child. Nancy was expecting in December.

Winter came early that year. Snow covered the ground and ice began to form on the trees. They had moved into the old cabin behind his folks home, planning to build a house of their own the following year.

The sleet had abated somewhat and Noah decided to gather the remaining pecans from the tree before the freeze ruined them. He took a large tow sack and headed to the tree, telling Nancy he'd be right back.

As he was gathering the nuts from the lower limbs that had been protected from the ice he had a strange feeling that he was being watched. The hair on his neck stood up and he felt goose bumps on his arms and knew they were not a result of the cold.

Suddenly, a figure appeared from behind the tree waving his arms and frowning. In an almost inaudible sound Noah could make out the words, "Go home, your wife needs you, go home!"

He lost no time in rushing to the cabin. As he entered the room he knew instinctively that something was wrong. He headed to the lean-to and found Nancy on the floor holding her stomach and crying out in pain. There was blood on the floor; she had lost their baby.

He picked her up in his arms and carried her to the four poster bed in the main cabin.

"I'm gonna get Momma. I'll be right back!" He was crying.

He rushed across the yard and through the back door, crying, "Momma! Momma! Something's wrong with Nancy! Come quick!"

His mother rushed to the cabin and knew at once what had happened. She sent Noah to find his pa and brother and to send Ben to Nancy's folks to fetch them.

Deborah did what she could to make Nancy comfortable, but she had lost too much blood. By the time Noah got back she was sinking fast. She took his hand in hers and whispered, "I'm so sorry."

She was dead when the others arrived. Noah was holding her in his arms rocking her back and forth as though she were a child. He was crying uncontrollably.

They buried her on the Knoll overlooking the hardwood forest not far from the pecan tree.

Noah soon moved back in with his folks. It would be years before he showed any interest in another woman.

The next year Ben married Nancy's younger sister, Olivia. They had twin boys the following year.

The Beacums continued to prosper, so much so that in 1859 Nath and Deborah built yet another, larger house a few hundred yards from the first one. Ben and Olivia moved into the old one. The ghost stories persisted, but

Noah never told his pa what had happened the day Nancy died.

Nath had acquired over five hundred acres by 1861, and life was looking good. Then war came to West Tennessee.

The Beacums, like most of their neighbors, never owned slaves and were staunch supporters of the Union. Ben even named his third child Abraham Lincoln.

Nath returned from his weekly visit to Lexington, the county seat, with disturbing news: though the majority of citizens in the county was opposed to secession, the state had wavered at the last minute and voted to join the confederacy.

Some prominent citizens were organizing a unit to serve in the Union army, the 7th Tennessee Cavalry. Nath was too old to serve, and Noah had injured his back two years before and could no longer sit a horse. Ben felt he had no choice. Southern sympathizers were already making things tough on the citizens loyal to the Union.

Olivia begged him not to go, but Ben would not be deterred. He took his best horse and his squirrel gun and rode off to join up with Captain Hayeworth in Lexington.

There were some minor skirmishes close to home as Forrest and his band foraged off the land. The sympathizers would point out the families that had men serving in the Union army and they would be on the receiving end of Forrest's brand of "justice."

The Beacum family did not escape untouched. Mavericks from Forrest's outfit burned the barn and stole all the animals. Only by burying the silverware and dishes did Deborah manage to save anything.

Forrest claimed to know nothing of this, but his men continued to terrorize the county.

Ben came home briefly in the spring of '62. He was only there for a few days when a courier arrived with orders for him to report to his unit, which had been ordered to Shiloh to join forces with General Grant.

Captain Asa Hayeworth led his men along the stage road that went from Lexington to Jackson, where they were placed under Lt. Col. Johnson's command and continued their journey south toward Savannah.

The weather was nice, spring was in the air, and wildflowers sent a riot of colors abounding along the trail.

There was an air of optimism among the troops. They felt that the confederates would never attack at Shiloh, for the navy had dozens of boats in the Tennessee River. They had no idea how wrong they were.

Johnson's regiment arrived near Savannah on Sunday afternoon and was hurriedly sent forward to report to General Grant. The Union had sustained great losses that morning at "the hornet's nest," so named later because the bullets flew so thick the soldiers on both sides said they were like angry hornets.

The troops' spirits were buoyed when word came that

the confederate commander, General Johnston had been killed that morning.

Preparations were made to join the battle the following morning. When the day ended, April seventh, almost eleven thousand confederate soldiers lay dead. The winner was the Union but at great loss of more than thirteen thousand men. Sergeant Ben Beacum was among the dead.

Nath Beacum was restless. It was late Monday night, April seventh, and he couldn't get Ben off his mind. Unable to sleep he slipped out of the house and walked down the path that led past the pecan tree.

The April moon was full, the sky was black as ebony, and the stars had a brilliance he'd never noticed before.

He was thinking back over the past quarter century since they had first settled here. Life had been good. He was approaching his sixty fifth birthday, and he should have been a happy man. He had wealth and a good wife and now three grandsons to carry on his name.

But tonight he was worried about his youngest son. He came to a large stump near the pecan tree and sat down to rest a spell. Suddenly, he felt as though someone was watching him. The hair on his neck stood on end, and a chill ran down his spine. That's when he felt the presence of someone. He looked up, and there under the boughs of the tree was a young boy, dressed in a tattered uniform that Nath didn't recognize. At first he thought it was one of Forrest's scavengers, but the boy had a sad look on his face, holding out his hands to Nath, and there were tears on his cheeks. His mouth formed the words, "I'm sorry." Then he was gone.

Nath hurriedly returned to the house. Deborah was sitting on the verandah waiting for him. She knew there was something wrong. He embraced her and with his voice choking said, "I know our boy is dead, I just know it."

Deborah cried softly into his massive shoulder. They stood for a long time embracing, finding strength in one another. Then without another word they went to bed.

The following week they received the bad news. Ben was dead.

Nath and Noah took the wagon to Jackson to retrieve Ben's body. The trip took three days. They managed to find enough ice to keep the body cool until they reached home.

Nath had never been one for religion, but he wanted someone to say a few words over his son. There was a small meeting house two miles away where a group calling themselves Christians Only worshipped. He knew most of them and had a respect for their religious zeal. He asked one of their elders to come over as they prepared to bury Ben on the hillside next to Noah's wife, Nancy.

As the minister spoke there was a rush of wind moving the leaves of the nearby pecan tree. Oddly, it wasn't blowing anywhere else. The air elsewhere was perfectly still.

Life went on at the Beacum farm. Nath was getting

too old to continue his peanut operation. He reluctantly turned it over to Noah, who didn't have his pa's business acumen.

CHAPTER THREE

In 1880 Nath was nearing eighty-three, and Deborah was almost eighty. Noah and Olivia had married ten years before, more as a matter of convenience than love. He loved his nephews and they loved him in return.

Ben's twins left in '79 to seek their fortunes further west. Little Nath and Little Samuel, named for their grandpas, went their separate ways after reaching St. Louis. Nath, always the adventurous one, went to Texas and joined the rangers. Three years later a gang member he had arrested the year before ambushed him.

They buried him in Texas.

Sam wound up in San Francisco and studied law, passing the bar at twenty-nine. He became quite successful, but tragedy struck when he drowned in a boating accident in the bay. The twins never had children.

Nath died in his sleep in eighteen ninety and a week later Deborah followed him in death. Noah knew his mother didn't want to live without Nath.

Link, as Ben's youngest came to be known, married a girl of social position in Jackson, but she could never adjust to country living. Besides, the Beacum wealth was slowly being reduced as one bad crop year followed another. She ran away with a drummer who was calling on Noah and Link to sell seeds for spring planting. Link missed her, but his momma thought, "Good riddance."

Through it all there were reports of strange happenings at the pecan tree. It was reported by a neighbor who had enjoyed the nuts in the past that when Nath and Deborah died the tree lost all its nuts. No one remembered picking up any at all that year.

The old tree was at least three feet in diameter by now but still green and healthy. After his wife ran away Link became more and more withdrawn. He'd spend days in his room, coming out only to get food or relieve himself.

Olivia and Noah couldn't seem to get through to him at all, hard as they tried. He eventually began to help around the farm, but the old spark was gone. It was almost as though the three of them were waiting to die.

Noah finally quit farming all together and found a renter to farm what had gradually become cotton land. He provided the seeds and took a third of the crops. This kept body and soul together but not much else.

The flu epidemic hit Henderson County in 1917 in a big way. It seemed that not a day passed that someone didn't die. More and more people reported strange happenings around the old pecan tree. Moving lights were a common occurrence, and once in awhile a coon hunter would swear he saw a young soldier with a sad look on his face.

Henderson County lost several sons in "the war to end all wars," and each time a soldier was laid to rest someone would report strange sights around the old tree.

Noah and Olivia both succumbed to the flu and Link never bothered to tell anyone. People had problems of their own. He took pine lumber that had been stored in the barn for years and made two rough caskets. Then he put the corpses in them and loaded them on the wagon and hauled them the short distance to the family graveyard. There he buried Noah between Nancy and Olivia.

He left the house now only to go the mile or so to the country grocery store once a week to buy food. He was not yet sixty years old, but he looked like a man of seventy-five.

At first, after his folks died, the neighbor women would prepare food and take it to him. He'd crack the front door and offer a weak, "Thank-you," but never invited them inside.

Once the preacher from the nearby church tried visiting but was rebuffed by Link who said, "My pa and grandpa never held much with religion, guess I don't either."

After that episode the preacher tried several times, but Link would hear his old hound dog Rattler barking, look outside to see who it was, and never come to the door.

The preacher stopped trying, saying, "The scripture says if they don't want to hear the Gospel then shake the dust off your feet and leave them alone."

Soon after, the ladies stopped bringing food. Somehow Link continued to survive. He had long since sold all the livestock, and now his tenant paid him annually with cash for rent of the land. He got enough to buy his groceries and at first to pay the taxes on the farm. The community came to know him as a hermit and a recluse. The townies just called him "crazy as a betsy-bug."

In 1938, exactly one hundred years since his grandpa had come over the mountains and settled this land, Link died. Mr. Wallace, who operated the grocery, missed him on his normal Saturday visit to buy food. He sent his son to check on him.

The door was open and the boy could see Link's body slumped over his old chair. He started back to get his pa and passed under the pecan tree. Suddenly he felt a cold wind blow through the boughs and a ragged boy about his age stepped from behind the large tree. He folded his hands and bowed his head, a tear formed on his cheek, then he was gone. Jamey Wallace had never run so fast in his life.

He breathlessly told his pa that Link was dead. Then he blurted out, "Pa, I seen the ghost, I did, he was no more'n five feet from me. He had a real sad look on his face and he was crying, then he just sorta disappeared."

"Now, boy, you was just scared 'cause you just seen your first dead man," Mr. Wallace tried to rationalize.

"No, I know what I seen and I seen the ghost." Jamey was adamant on that point.

The neighbors came with a coffin from Pafford's Funeral Home. The men dressed the body and laid it in the casket. They buried Link next to his pa. The minister who had tried so hard to talk with Link in life had the unpleasant task of saying a few words before the burial.

It was early fall and still warm, but there was a sudden chill over the grave site, and those present swore later that the big old pecan tree swayed in the wind though the air was still.

CHAPTER FOUR

The next year the old Beacum place was sold on the courthouse steps in Lexington for back taxes. There was only a little over one hundred acres remaining of Nath and Deborah's original five hundred acres. Over the years, first Noah, then Link had found an easy way to supplement their revenue by selling a few acres at a time to eager buyers.

Ronald Logan was a twenty-four year old school teacher, recently arrived in Lexington with his wife, Pamela, and six year old son, Josh. He had earned a teaching certificate while working as an accountant for a large firm in Memphis. He gave up that promising career and moved to Henderson County because he wanted Josh to experience the kind of childhood he and Pamela had enjoyed growing up in a small town in east Arkansas.

He had a teaching contract for the year at the two-room elementary school near the Beacum farm. He was paid an additional fifty dollars a month to fill the job of principal as well. This meant he taught fifth through eighth grade while old Mrs. Duncan taught first through fourth grades. The total enrollment was only fifty children.

He and Pam decided to use the nest egg they'd saved to bid on the farm. He couldn't believe it when he was the high bidder. He got a hundred acres of prime farmland, grown over and not much to look at, to be sure, but the big house was livable and the four thousand dollars he spent was a bargain.

"We've got everything we ever wanted," thought Ron. "Nothing can happen to us now." How wrong he was.

Times were still hard in west Tennessee. If the Depression was over someone forgot to tell the citizens of Henderson County.

The day the Logans prepared to take their meager belongings and move to the farm, they were surprised to find the neighbors and the ladies from the little church already there with food and everything they needed to get the house in a livable condition.

"Well, folks, we're sure glad to have someone move in this old place." Ed Johnson, the nearest neighbor, said. "The house is well built and just needs some sprucing up," he continued.

This was just the sort of thing they had missed living in the city. "How can we ever repay you?" an astonished Ron asked.

"That's what neighbors are for," Mrs. Johnson joined in.

"Love thy neighbor as thy self, the Bible says," added the minister. "These folks take that literally."

After three days of labor and lots of help from the neighbors the house was restored to something of its former beauty. Mr. Johnson was right — it was well built and in good shape.

Pam had noticed the beautiful old pecan tree the first day they visited the farm. "Oh, honey, it's so big and beautiful." she had told Ron.

It was May 1939 and the tree was clothed in green leaves and thousands of tiny flowers that would become pecans. She asked some of the ladies who were helping to clean up the house, "How old do you think that pecan tree is?" They had pecans trees in Arkansas, but she'd never seen one this big.

The preacher's wife looked at Mrs. Johnson with a half smile on her face. "Some say it's more than a hundred and twenty years old. It was supposedly planted by a soldier in Andrew Jackson's army when they returned from the battle at New Orleans."

Mrs. Johnson wiped her hands on her apron and looked around to see if her husband or the preacher was within earshot. Satisfied they couldn't hear she said, "There's a legend that says a soldier boy was killed on that spot, and the pecan tree grew from his grave. Lots of folks say it's haunted."

The preacher's wife seemed uncomfortable. "The Bible says there are things we don't understand, and I think this is one of them," she continued. "My husband don't hold to any ghost stories, but I know some strange things have been seen around that tree."

Pam laughed. "Ladies, if you're trying to scare me you're doing a good job."

"No, honey, we didn't mean to do that. But sooner or later you're going to hear stories. We just thought it would be better if you knew."

That night after they put Josh to bed Pam told Ron about her discussion with the ladies about the pecan tree. "Let's go down there right now and see if anything strange happens," she begged.

"Okay. Josh should be asleep by now. We might as well put this nonsense to rest right now," he said.

The late spring sky was dazzling with stars, and as they left the house the huge yellow moon peeked over the eastern horizon. The full moon made them both homesick for their Arkansas farms.

As they approached the big tree a dog howled in the distance and a hoot owl announced his presence as he prepared to forage for his supper. They both felt a chill up their spines but were determined to complete their mission.

Pam snuggled against Ron and he put his arm around her. "There's absolutely nothing to fear Mrs. Logan, I'll protect you with my life," he joked.

They found a grassy spot near the tree and sat down, she with her head on his shoulder and he with his arms embracing her. They talked of their future and how blessed they were to have such caring neighbors. They decided to visit the little church Sunday.

An hour passed and Pam said, "We really need to go and check on Josh. If he wakes up and we aren't there he might be frightened."

Ron was ready to go, too, but for an entirely different reason. With all that had been happening, he and Pam hadn't had much time to call their own, and he had plans of his own for tonight.

Just as they got up and started for the house they felt a cold breeze blowing on them. They turned to look at the tree and there were lights that seemed to float in the air. They both said later that their eyes played a trick on them, and that really wasn't a boy in uniform that seemed to materialize from behind the tree and just as quickly disappear.

Regardless of whether or not the tree was indeed haunted didn't stop them from restoring the house and barn. They bought a cow, some chickens, and a couple of hogs. They planted a garden but didn't have time or equipment to plant a crop of cotton. Mr. Johnson gladly paid cash rent for ninety acres.

1939 was a good year for the Logan family. Even though the country was still in the throes of the Depression, Ron and Pam prospered with lots of hard work and frugal living. They placed membership with the nearby church and both were put to work teaching Sunday school classes. Josh thrived on the country life. He made friends easily and did well in school.

1940 was an uneventful year. Mr. Johnson had another bumper crop of cotton, and by this time the Logans were planting five acres in tomatoes, squash, corn, and okra. They had a ready market in town at the grocery stores.

They began to make plans for Pam to attend teachers college at Austin Peay in Clarksville. It would be tough. Clarksville was seventy miles away, but they were determined that next year she would do it.

1941 promised to be a repeat of the previous two years, but the politicians in Washington had different plans. The country continued in the Depression after all those years, and no amount of government programs was going to resolve the problem.

The answer was simple to the "powers that be": involve the country in a war and put everyone to work making war materiel and the Depression would disappear. The fact that people would die was an acceptable alternative to the professional politicians in the capitol.

CHAPTER FIVE

December 7, 1941 forever changed the lives of millions of Americans including the Logan family. After word of Pearl Harbor came the public clamored to join the military and demanded that we strike back at Japan.

Ron weighed his responsibilities. Josh was not quite ten years old and he felt his first obligation was to him and Pam. But he felt an overwhelming need to serve his country.

"Honey, I don't expect you to understand, but this is something I have to do."

He tried to console Pam. He hugged her and then turned to Josh. "Son, sometimes there are things that are bigger than we are. I hope you'll understand. Besides, I'll be home before you know it."

Josh wasn't buying it, but he knew his dad loved him and if he said he had to go to war then Josh would accept that regardless of the fear he had.

On December eighth Ron caught the bus to Jackson and enlisted in the army. After only twelve weeks of basic training in Camp Rucker, Alabama, he was on his way to Fort Lewis, Washington. He got a week's leave to spend with his family. From Ft. Lewis he boarded a troop ship with thousands of other raw recruits bound for the Philippines. He landed on March twenty first, his twenty-eighth birthday.

Things happened quickly during the first months of the war. His company was sent at once to the island of Luzon to help the American-Filipino forces as the Japanese overran them. His platoon lieutenant and platoon sergeant were mortally wounded the first day of fighting. He rallied the platoon and they held their ground. He received a wound to his arm but kept encouraging the men to stand and fight.

A week after landing he was given a battlefield commission as second lieutenant.

The Japanese army overran their position and he was taken prisoner along with his platoon and thousands of other Americans.

Back home all the news was about the terrible atrocities that the Japanese were committing against the Americans. They were force-marched in what became known as the Bataan Death March. One by one Ron watched as his fellow soldiers were brutalized. There was never enough food, and though some individual guards tried to make life a little easier, for the most part they seemed to enjoy the cruelty to the soldiers.

It was April 1942, when the Japanese took thirty-seven thousand soldiers on that awful march. Josh was on his way to the creek to fish on a Saturday afternoon when he stopped under the big pecan tree to rest. He lay on the fallen leaves from the year before and closed his eyes. "I sure miss Dad," he thought, choking back his tears. The air was still and the afternoon sun shone like a bright light in the blue sky. Suddenly he felt a chill and sat upright.

There, next to the huge trunk, was a boy in tattered clothes. At first he thought it was one of the many Ledbetter kids from across the creek. They were never too clean. Then the boy moved closer and hung his head moving it back and forth with a sad look on his face. Then just as quickly he disappeared behind the tree.

Still, Josh thought it was a Ledbetter. He got up and looked behind the tree but no one was there.

He forgot about fishing and ran quickly to the house, shouting, "Mom! Mom! Something's happened to Dad! I just know it!" He fell into his mom's arms and began to sob uncontrollably.

"What is it, honey, why are you so upset?"

"I saw him, Mom, I saw the ghost boy and he looked so sad. Then he — he just disappeared. He was trying to tell me something bad has happened to Dad," he sobbed.

Pam held him for a long time just like when he was a baby. Finally they ate a little supper and went to bed. Josh prayed over and over for Jesus to protect his dad.

The next day Pam got the news about Ron when the county sheriff drove out. She had not had a letter since he first landed in the Philippines. She didn't know about his commission.

"Pam, I'm so sorry," said Sheriff Roberts, whose own son was somewhere in Europe. "I have a telegram from the war department for you." He was teary eyed.

"Were are sorry to report," she read, "that Lt. Ronald Logan is missing in action and presumed dead."

Pam was in shock. She couldn't believe what she was reading.

She continued: "Lt. Logan rallied his platoon when his platoon lieutenant and sergeant were killed and showed himself to be a brave and effective leader. He was given a battlefield commission the day before his presumed death. You can take great pride in the service your husband provided to his country." It was signed by a Captain King in the war department in Washington D.C.

"What's wrong, Mom?" asked Josh as he came out of the house. "It's about Dad, isn't it? I told you something happened to him. The ghost boy wanted me to know."

Sheriff Roberts had an inquisitive look on his face. "Did you say you saw the ghost down at the pecan tree, Josh?"

"Yes, sir. I was resting yesterday and thought I fell asleep, but I knew I didn't. What's happened, Mom?" he begged to be answered.

Sheriff Roberts remembered the time he'd been coon hunting and saw the boy looking sad. When he got home his wife told him his dad had died.

Pam sat down on the porch and pulled Josh to her. "Honey, Sheriff Roberts brought a telegram from the war department. Your dad is missing in action." She couldn't bring herself to tell him his dad was presumed dead.

"Pam, is there anything I can do for you and Josh?" the big man asked in a trembling voice bordering on tears.

"No, no, we'll be alright," she replied. "I think I'll call Mrs. Johnson and ask her to spend the night with us."

"I'll get back to town then. Call my wife if you need me." He made her promise.

CHAPTER SIX

The next three years slowly passed. Josh was almost thirteen and going through puberty.

"Now is when he needs his dad most," thought Pam. Her folks and Ron's called frequently. She had gone back to Arkansas shortly after the telegram arrived, but she missed Ron so much and she felt closer to him at home. Besides, Josh had to get back in school after the cotton was chopped.

She and Josh continued to raise the truck crops that, with the check the army sent, took care of their basic needs. She put her plans for school on indefinite hold.

There was another early winter in the fall of '44, but just as quickly spring began to make itself known in early February.

"Mom, I'll go bring the cows to the barn. It looks like rain," said Josh.

"O.K, honey, but hurry. It's just too hot for February. We could have a tornado," she warned.

He put on a short sleeve shirt and his ball cap and began running toward the pasture beside the pecan tree. "Hope it don't start to storm till I get the cows in the barn," he thought wistfully.

Just as he approached the tree he felt a chill down his

spine, like he felt three years ago. His instincts were right on the money. The boy in the ragged uniform appeared from nowhere next to the big tree. This time he was smiling, his gaunt face twisted as he nodded his head, and Josh could make out the words, "It's gonna be all right. Don't be afraid."

Then, as before so long ago, he was gone. This time Josh didn't bother to look behind the tree. He knew this was not a Ledbetter.

He hurriedly drove the two milch cows to the shelter of the barn just as lightning streaked across the dark sky and thunder rolled across the fields.

He rushed into the house as the clouds opened up and loosed the torrential rains. "Mom! Mom!" he called excitedly. "Mom, Dad's o.k. I know he is, the ghost boy just told me." He was beside himself with excitement.

Pam thought he was delirious. "Honey, what's wrong?" I know you miss your dad, but we have to accept the fact that he's not coming home, ever." She began to cry.

"No, Mom, no. He's all right. I just know it. The ghost boy told me not to worry. Everything is gonna be o.k."

Just as she reached to take him in her arms there was a loud explosion and the sky became as bright as day. Looking toward the pecan tree where the noise seemed to come from they both saw an awesome sight.

"Wow, Mom, look at that! Lightning struck the pecan tree and it's on fire." He couldn't believe his eyes.

They stood mesmerized by the sight. The big tree was still bare from winter and some of the branches were dead. It wasn't long before the entire trunk, split down the middle by the lightning strike, was totally consumed.

The storm moved on as quickly as it had appeared, though it continued to rain steadily all night. Pam wanted to believe what Josh had said, but it made no sense. Surely his imagination had played a trick on him. Then she remembered almost three years ago what had happened before the sheriff delivered the telegram.

"Let's eat some supper and go to bed early," she suggested.

"Okay, Mom." He didn't argue.

Josh was restless. He tossed and turned a very long time before sleep came. He was dreaming about his dad coming home when an eerie blue light bathed his room from some unknown source.

He opened his eyes slowly, still thinking he was dreaming. There, sitting on the foot of his bed, was the young soldier. His hair was wet as well as his uniform. He smiled. "Your dad's coming home, and I'm going home at last," he said in a clear voice that Josh had no trouble understanding.

Josh rubbed his eyes. This was the strangest dream he'd ever had. The boy continued, "I fit at the battle at

N'Orleans with Old Hickory."

Strangely, Josh wasn't afraid of this apparition or dream or whatever it was.

"I ain't seen my maw and paw for a long time. They shot me and buried me here. Then they all went home."

"Your pa's comin' home, just you wait an' see. He's comin' home." With that he walked toward the door and as the blue light faded so did he.

Josh sat up in his bed. "That sure was a strange dream, but I sure wish it'd come true," he thought.

He decided to wait until morning to tell his mom. She would just feel his forehead to see if he was feverish. He turned over and finally went back to sleep.

Before dawn the old rooster crowed, heralding the beginning of a new day. Josh stirred and sat up, trying to remember as much about his dream as he could, to tell his mom.

He rolled over and stood up, stepping into something wet and sticky on the floor. He looked down, knowing his feet had been dry the night before. There were muddy prints of bare feet on the rug.

A chill ran over his body. He turned to look at his clock, and there on the nightstand was a large pecan. When he got to the kitchen his mom was humming as she prepared breakfast. "What you humming for?" he asked.

"We had a visit from Sheriff Roberts and a man from

the army office in Jackson after you were asleep last night." She smiled and pulled a telegram from her apron pocket. She handed it to him.

He read, "It is with a great deal of pleasure that we hereby inform you that Lt. Ronald Logan was among the survivors found when troops of General MacArthur liberated the American prisoners from Bataan. Lt. Logan is en route to Fort Lewis, Washington, where he will be treated for mal-nourishment and should be home in thirty days. Please do not attempt to make the trip to Ft. Lewis, as you would be unable to see him.

"The war department."

Josh told his mom about his dream that wasn't a dream. Then he showed her the pecan. They both went to the tool shed and got a shovel. As they emerged from the tool shed the sun burst over the eastern horizon with a brilliance Pam had not noticed in a long time.

"It's going to be beautiful day, Josh," she said, hugging her son tightly.

"I have a feeling the young soldier is with his folks this morning at last," she added.

"Mom, let's plant this pecan closer to the house. I think he would like that," said a very happy Josh.

They dug in silence, then Josh placed the pecan in the hole and they covered it with the rich soil.

"We'll always think of the young soldier when we look at the pecan tree," Pam said.

They walked hand in hand back inside to breakfast. It was indeed the beginning of a beautiful day.

Note: This story was based on an actual event taken from The Indian Wars. Andrew Jackson ordered a 16 year old boy shot when he refused to obey an order given by his sergeant.

A CHRISTMAS REMEMBERED

December, 1958, Giessen, Germany

It was quite a cultural shock, as well as a weather and climate shock, when our troop ship docked in Bremen, Germany, in November 1958. We boarded a train in the cold drizzle and arrived at our "home away from home," Ayers Kaserne, located on a hill overlooking the little hamlet of Kirch Goens.

It was late at night when I finally made it to D Company, 2nd Armored Rifle Battalion, Combat Command A, Third Armored Division, "Spearhead". The mess hall had remained open to feed us a hot meal before we finally went to bed about midnight. This would be home for the next eighteen months, so I set about learning what was expected of me.

I had been accepted at Officer Candidate School while at Fort Hood, Texas but was shipped out before I enrolled. I was given the opportunity to go back to Fort Benning, Georgia, for six months of training and then return to Spearhead as a second lieutenant. I was interested until I learned it meant an additional enlistment of three years. Suddenly, being an enlisted man didn't seem all that bad.

It was getting close to Christmas and many of us were homesick, when we discovered that our battalion supported an orphanage a few miles away, in the city of Giessen. It was a custom for volunteer soldiers to visit the orphans and take them gifts. I immediately volunteered to go. We loaded on a large truck carrying gifts and food from the mess hall. We even had a Santa Claus, a rotund soldier, who needed no padding. He was the perfect Kris Kringle!

To appreciate our experience one needs to understand something of the political climate during the "cold war". We had trained for six months in Texas on military tactics, which are designed, for only one purpose: to teach you how to kill another human being. At that time in Germany there was literally a communist spy under ever bed, so to speak.

We were on alert a good part of the time. We had to be very careful when on leave and associating with the local citizens. We never knew who our friends were or who was an East German spy trying to gather any scrap of information from whatever source available.

We put our concerns aside as we arrived at the Orphanage and entered the building. It was supported by the West German government but was actually run by a group of Roman Catholic nuns, with the added help of donations made every payday by some of us.

The large room was brightly decorated and the children were ecstatic. There were several nuns on hand to keep order. The soldiers were having as much fun as the kids, as hugs were exchanged and eyes filled with tears. Some of the men had small children back home and this was really hard for them, but they shared their love with these children, many of whom were fathered by American soldiers. Those soldiers returned home after their time was up, and the mothers put the children in the home to avoid embarrassment. This was particularly difficult for the kids whose dads were black Americans.

As the day wore on I noticed a little fellow about six years old who wasn't taking part in the festivities. He would remain in a corner away from the crowd. I asked one of the nuns about him and in her broken English she explained: his parents had attempted to escape from East Germany or Czechoslovakia, and were shot to death by the communist border guards. He was found wandering around in a field. When he arrived at the orphanage he refused to speak and they gave him the name Hans. He had been there for quite some time and had never uttered a word, nor showed any emotion.

I began trying to communicate with him. At first he tried to ignore my smiles and gestures but finally started to watch my every move. When I felt the time was right I approached him and kneeling down I stretched out my arms to him. Suddenly, he ran to me putting his arms around me and snuggling his face to mine.

One of the nuns came over with tears in her eyes and said that was the first time he had shown any emotion. He held on to me for the rest of the day. Though he still didn't speak, there was no doubt that he had not forgotten how to give or receive love.

Too soon the day was over and we loaded onto the truck as the children gathered in the yard. They began to sing, "Stille Nacht, Heilige Nacht." We responded by singing in English, "Silent Night, Holy Night." I will never forget that scene, a bunch of hardened soldiers and those wonderful children singing together. Our own languages may have been different, but our hearts were intertwined.

I have enjoyed many Christmases since then with my children and now my grandchildren, but there is a special feeling I have every Christmas as I remember Hans and the other children. That is a Christmas I will never forget.

MIDSUMMER MEMORIES

Lying on my back on a grassy knoll in mid-July, a ten-year-old dreamer.

The cumulus clouds piled so high in the deep blue sky they look like a medieval castle.

There's a white puffy elephant being ridden by a boy about my age, chased by a lion.

The lion slowly evolves into a clown complete with a big nose and a funny hat.

The hot southern wind blows over my face as only a West Tennessee wind can do.

The cotton has been chopped and school doesn't start for a few more days.

What better way to spend the free time than creating a place of wonder in the clouds?

The sky darkens as the ominous sound of thunder rolls across the open spaces.

Lightning zigzags across the sky creating a natural light show.

The spell broken, I head for shelter. The funny creations from high piled clouds must wait for another day.

One day I awake and realize the aging face in the mirror belongs to me; where did the time go?

What happened to my dreams of far away places and exotic lands?

I reach deep into the recesses of my mind and enter a musty cellar of memories.

I pull a box off a shelf marked "Fragile, handle with care." I open it carefully and relive the happy experiences all over again.

You see, nothing is ever lost if we keep the key to the rusty lock of our memories.

SEASONS OF LIFE, CYCLES OF LOVE

As the year contains four seasons, so too, does the cycle of love and marriage.

When you fall in love your name becomes, "Honey." This is a time of wonder and passion for the one you want to spend your whole life with.

"I love you, honey."

When the children come, as they inevitably do, your name transitions to daddy. What a wonderful time of life this is.

"Who made the moon, Daddy? How big is the world, Daddy?"

"I love you, Daddy."

Horror of horrors, the children become teenagers and you become the more somber, "Dad."

"Please don't say anything to embarrass me in front of my friends, Dad."

"My best friend's dad is cool, why do you have to dress like that, Dad?"

"Can I borrow the car, dad, we're going to the mall and I'm the only one who can drive."

It's not cool to say, "I love you, Dad."

For most of us our Creator finally rewards us
for surviving the terrible teen years
by giving us grandchildren.

The cycle is complete, now we're "PawPaw."

"Ride me on your shoulders, PawPaw,
please, just one more time."

"I want some ice cream, PawPaw,
will you take me to Baskin-Robbins?"

"I love you so-o-o-o much, PawPaw."

For the blessed among us,
when the cycle is complete, it starts all over again.

"Honey, I'm calling the grandkids,
do you want to talk to them?"

"Honey, I'm going to the mall, do you want to come along? "Don't rush me if you do."

Sitting together in the living room on a Sunday afternoon, the fires of passion have dwindled, but they have been replaced with something far more precious and enduring.

She knows what you're going to say before you say it. You know how much she loves you without asking.

Though the firm skin has given way to wrinkles and the thinning hair is turning gray, the intimacy has grown over the years.

Back through the foggy corridors of time,
memories surface.

"Do you take this woman...?"

Those vows taken before man and God still ring true in your memory and you realize you have lived and loved and been loved.

As surely as the springtime comes with it's refreshing rain and re-creation of life, so too, must the winter come when nature sleeps and prepares for a new year.

When our winter comes and we sleep,
we have the hope of a glorious resurrection and
eternal springtime with our Creator.

SEPTEMBER 11, 2001

A DAY OF INFAMY

An open letter to my grandsons, Joshua and Logan Britt:

I love you both very much. This has been a very difficult time for me and, I'm sure, for you as well. Not in our wildest imagination could we ever have thought such a thing could happen in America!

When tragedies such as this occur we sometimes wonder why a loving God would allow it to happen. We must remember that He set natural law in place when He created the earth. When human beings violate that law, bad things happen.

I pray that our leaders will be able to bring the evil people, responsible for this to justice. I pray it can be done without sacrificing the lives of our young soldiers as well as innocent people in foreign lands.

I pray for you both everyday that we can enjoy a measure of peace as you grow to manhood. I also pray that you will study the Bible for yourselves and come to an understanding of what God requires of a Christian in times such as these.

As His children it is not for us to seek vengeance against others. If a Christian is called to serve his country he should do so proudly, but he is not required to take another human life. Some of our greatest heroes in past wars were men whose conscience would not allow them to kill. They served as medics on the battlefield and orderlies in the hospitals, and they served their country well without taking a life.

Our Savior is the Prince of Peace, not of war.

You are in the springtime of your lives as I enter the winter season of mine. I have been blessed with a good wife and children and grandchildren

Remember how much I love you. Be kind to everyone you encounter on your journey through life. No one is better than anyone else. God made us all in His image.

Life is meant to be celebrated and enjoyed, especially by Christians, so, enjoy.

Your devoted grandfather.

FAR FROM HOME

The cold, gray waters of the Atlantic
slowly separate us from home.

An era has ended and a new one is about to begin.
We're no longer children.

Four thousand ruddy-faced boy-men
share a troop ship bound for Europe.

Some will be there for eighteen months, others
much longer, all about to face life.

Winters are harsh in Germany.
Sleeping on the frozen,
snow-covered ground isn't easy.

A sponge bath and a shave with water from
thawed ice in a steel helmet, now a luxury.

World War II - C-rations, fifteen years old, heated
over an open fire, taste like gourmet food
when you're hungry.

Boiling, hot coffee in an aluminum canteen cup,
turning ice cold before it can be consumed.

Four feet of snow and ten below zero on the
East German border, at the height of the cold war.

Forced marches at midnight, learning to read a map
and compass. School didn't prepare us for this.

After two months of Hell it's back to the barracks
and some semblance of civilization.

And how we've changed. The ruddy-faced boys are
now men, ready to do a man's job.

Prom night and graduation day only a few months
in the past, when we were still boys.

A well earned weekend pass and a trip to the city,
bars, drinks, and girls. So this is life.

After an eternity and more of the same the ship
traverses the Atlantic once more, home to America.

Who are these worldly warriors aboard, and what
happened to the innocent boys?

The faces are now of men. Some are hardened by
the experience; others learned compassion and
kindness.

What will the future hold for these young men?
They have learned to survive anything.

Will life be good to us?
Will our sweethearts be waiting?

Only time will tell.
We left these shores in innocence
and returned worldly men.

Forty-five years have passed
and none of the dreams came true.

Forty-five years have passed and
life gave many unexpected pleasures.

A mate to love and children who brought happiness
along with pain.

The winter of life is fast approaching, and memories
from the past re-appear.

The face in the mirror doesn't fit
the young man inside. What has happened?

Why must nature play such cruel tricks?
That can't be me staring back from the glass.

Before sleep there is always reflection and prayer.

Did I do more good than harm on my way through
life? Did I pick someone up who was down?

I taught my children that love, mercy, and compassion were the important things in life.

My success in life will be measured by
how well they received my teaching.

My reward is knowing that my God is a God of
mercy and forgiveness, and I look forward to
seeing Him face to face.

May those who know me best
reflect on their relationship with me and smile.

FOREVER FRIENDS

Morgan, the little gray mouse, was excited. She had just returned home after a week at her grandma's house and she was looking forward to telling her best friend, Kaitlyn Caterpillar, about her visit. Her mom and dad had brought back large quantities of fresh milk and yellow cheese from Farmer Brown's dairy barn where her grandma lived.

"Mom, Dad, may I go now? I haven't seen Kaitlyn for over a week," she begged. The Caterpillar family made their home in the big mulberry tree in the center of the meadow that bordered the forest where Morgan lived.

"Help your mom put the food away and you can go for a little while," her dad said with a smile.

She quickly helped her mother take the food to the kitchen, then, running out the front door she said, "I'll be home soon."

Wild rose bushes and milkweed shaded the path across the meadow. She passed a large family of honeybees feasting on the nectar from the wild roses. "Hello, Morgan," they called. She waved with one hand while holding her new straw hat to her head with the other. The wind was strong and she didn't want to lose the gift her Grandma had made for her.

A little further along she saw the ladybug family enjoying the tender leaves of the milkweed. "We've missed you, Morgan," they called.

"Thanks. It's good to be home."

The Lizard family was enjoying the sun as they napped on a large flat rock. They barely moved as she ran past.

She reached the stream that ran through the middle of the meadow. Luckily, Mr. Benjamin Butterworth Bullfrog III was nearby. She didn't want to get her feet wet.

"Climb aboard, Morgan," he said in his velvety baritone voice. "I haven't seen you for awhile."

"I've been visiting my grandma. We just got home," she replied.

"I know Kaitlyn will be glad to see you," he said as he glided across the stream.

As he neared the other side he just couldn't resist taking one jump. After all, that's what bullfrogs do best. He landed on the bank, but not before splashing water all over Morgan.

"I'm sorry I got you all wet, Morgan," he apologized.

"That was fun. My dress will dry," she giggled.

She ran along the path and finally reached the mulberry tree. "Kaitlyn, it's me. Where are you?" She looked under the leaves and there was no one there. "Where is the Caterpillar family?" she asked of no one in particular.

The leaves were bare, but hanging from the limbs were

many gray, pod-looking things held up by silk threads. Morgan was frightened. She thought she saw one of them move. That's all it took. She turned and ran as fast as she could back toward the stream. The wind took her new hat off her head, but she never noticed.

"Mr. Bullfrog," she cried, "where are you?"

"Morgan, what's wrong?" he asked, climbing up on the bank.

She was in tears. "Kaitlyn and everybody are gone," she cried.

"Now, now, it's not as bad as you think. Hop on and I'll get you across the stream. Then your Mom can tell you what has happened."

He quickly swam across the stream and made it to the other side. This time he resisted the urge to see how far he could jump.

"Mom! Dad!" she cried breathlessly as she ran into the house. "Something's happened to Kaitlyn and her family. They're all gone." She spoke so fast they could barely tell what she was talking about.

"Slow down, dear," her mother said. "Catch your breath. We can hardly tell what you're saying."

"Kaitlyn's gone, Mom. They're all gone. There are some strange looking pods hanging from the limbs. I'm afraid they ate Kaitlyn," she cried.

"No, dear, nothing has eaten Kaitlyn. Come sit down. I have something to tell you," her mother said gently.

"What has happened, Mom? Where's Kaitlyn?"

"Your father and I should have prepared you for this," she said softly. "But it happened early this year, and with us gone on vacation it just slipped our minds."

"What happened?" Morgan asked, with tears streaming down her face.

"Well, dear, every year something strange and wonderful happens to the Caterpillars," Mrs. Mouse said softly.

"What, Mom? What happens?" She was insistent.

"You will have to play alone for awhile and trust us," her mom answered mysteriously.

"Why can't you tell me now?" she yelled.

"It is such a wonderful miracle I can't really describe it. Please trust your dad and me, and you will be pleasantly surprised," she promised.

"I believe the Chipmunk family that just moved in the old place down the road have a daughter about your age. You can make friends with her," her mom added.

"I'll go meet her, but no one can take Kaitlyn's place. She and I will be friends forever," she answered sadly.

After dinner Morgan sat in her room feeling sad. She remembered the first time she met Kaitlyn. She was playing alone under the mulberry tree while her mom picked some fresh seeds from the nutgrass.

"Hi," came a small voice from nowhere. Morgan looked around but saw no one. Then she heard the voice again. "My name is Kaitlyn. What's yours?"

Morgan looked up and saw the cutest little worm she had ever seen. Startled, she answered, "I'm Morgan. I live just across the meadow."

"Would you like to be friends?" asked the little worm. "I'm a Caterpillar."

"I guess so. Can you come to my house to play?" Morgan asked.

"No, I have to stay near the mulberry tree for several weeks. I don't know why."

"I come over to the meadow almost every day and play while my mom gathers food. We can visit then," said an excited Morgan.

"That will be lots of fun," Kaitlyn said, smiling. "We'll have lots of time to play and talk before something happens," she continued.

"Why won't someone tell you what's going to happen?" asked Morgan.

"I don't really know, except they said it would be something wonderful," Kaitlyn replied.

The days turned into weeks, and they became the very best of friends. Morgan never questioned Kaitlyn again. Rather, she decided she would just enjoy their friendship and let the future take care of itself.

"Now," she thought, "it's too late. I wish I hadn't gone to Grandma's."

A week passed as Morgan moped around her room. She had gone to meet the Chipmunks with her mom, but it just wasn't the same without Kaitlyn.

"All right, young lady, enough of this," her mom said. "It's time you got out of the house and enjoyed the sunshine."

With that she put a basket in Morgan's hand and said, "I don't have time to gather any nuts today. You'll have to go by yourself."

"But, Mom, I don't want to go by myself," she begged.

But her mom wouldn't give in. "Run along so you can get back for lunch."

She took the basket reluctantly. "It makes me sad to go to the mulberry tree," she told her mother. "Can't I go somewhere else?" she begged.

"No, that's the only place where the nutgrass grows, and I need the nuts for supper" she said, unrelenting.

Morgan slowly wandered down the path toward the stream. She passed the Bee family and the Ladybug family, but she barely waved.

Benjamin Butterworth Bullfrog III was napping on the bank of the stream. He awoke when she called his name.

"Well, young lady, I haven't seen you for quite sometime," his voice boomed.

"I know. I miss Kaitlyn so much I've just stayed in my room."

"Well, hop aboard and I'll get you across without getting you wet this time," he promised.

She thanked him as they reached the other bank. She slid off his back to the ground and continued on her way half-heartedly.

As she approached the mulberry tree she thought she heard a voice that sounded like Kaitlyn. "I must be hearing things," she thought.

"Hi, Morgan. Look up here." She definitely heard a voice that time.

She shaded her eyes from the morning sun and looked up. She couldn't believe her eyes. It appeared that her new straw hat was flying overhead.

"Morgan, it's me, Kaitlyn," said the hat.

She was determined not to be afraid or to run. "Where are you?" she asked

Suddenly, her hat began to fall to the earth, revealing the most beautiful butterfly she had ever seen. It had delicate blue wings and was no bigger than Morgan.

She was stunned and confused until the butterfly lit on the milkweed within inches of her face. Morgan could hardly believe her eyes. She was staring into the face of her long lost friend, Kaitlyn.

"Oh, Kaitlyn," she cried as she rushed to hug her.

"I've missed you so much. What has happened to you?" She was breathless.

"Slow down," said Kaitlyn, returning her hug. "I've missed you, too."

"It happened just the way I heard. I was wrapped in silk threads, and when I finally got out I was no longer a caterpillar. I'm a butterfly!" she said all in one breath.

Morgan was so surprised and happy she began to cry. "I saw those cocoons hanging from the tree and I thought something had eaten you," she said. "You...you're beautiful," she stammered.

"Why, thank-you, Morgan." Kaitlyn replied.

"Come on, Kaitlyn. I want you to meet my friends, starting with Mr. Bullfrog, and then I want you to go home with me, please." Morgan had never been this excited before.

She picked up her straw hat and put it on her head. "My grandma made this for me, but I lost it when I ran home after I couldn't find you."

Kaitlyn flapped her delicate wings and flew above Morgan as they headed toward the stream. "We're never going to be apart again. We'll be friends forever."

HIGH WIRE HERO

Logan was excited. Tomorrow he would be twelve years old. "I sure hope I get a new bike," he thought wistfully. His bike, second-hand when he got it three years before, had finally worn out.

As he anticipated his long awaited birthday, he prepared for his daily practice on the high wire. Logan's grandfather, a high wire artist, had traveled the world with the circus. Billed as "The Great Gambino," Arthur Gamble's name had been a household word until the fall that left him crippled for life.

"Papaw has lived with us since Grandma died, when I was three," Logan told his best friend, Joey. "He taught me to walk the high wire when I was five." Logan knew his grandpa hoped he would follow in his footsteps someday.

Logan's dad, Walter, chose not to follow the circus, becoming instead a boring accountant, as Papaw would say, with a hint of disappointment in his voice.

His parents wanted Logan to become a doctor, but Papaw would remind his only grandson that the circus was making a comeback. "Logan, if you'll discipline yourself and practice everyday, you'll be as good at eighteen as I was in my prime. If I'd practiced more," he added sorrowfully, "maybe I'd never have fallen."

Logan idolized Papaw, and he practiced everyday, even when it meant he had no time for other things. Joey kidded him about not playing Little League, but there was not enough time to do everything he'd like to.

Logan was thankful for Joey Wesson's friendship and they spent a lot of time together. Joey's grandparents lived on the street behind Logan's house, and he stayed with them everyday until his parents got off work. Grandpa Wesson had even helped Walter string the heavy cable between their houses and across the narrow stream that separated the two backyards for Logan to practice on.

Walking the thirty yards or so between the houses, ten feet above the ground was exciting, especially after a rainstorm when the normally calm stream below became a torrent of rushing water and debris.

It seemed the stream stayed full this July because of the frequent rainstorms. Today was no different. The weatherman kept warning of impending storms. They were predicting heavy rain with high winds and lots of lightning.

Logan was about to mount the wire when Mr. Wesson called from the kitchen window, "Joey, Grandma is out of insulin. I'm going to the drugstore to pick it up. If it starts to rain, don't cross the stream. I'll pick you up in front of Logan's house."

"O.K., Grandpa," Joey replied, "I'll be watching for you."

No sooner had Mr. Wesson sped off to the pharmacy

than it began to rain. Black clouds boiled over angrily as they were tossed about by the wind. The bright afternoon sun soon gave way to continual flashes of lightning. The thunder sounded more ominous than ever before.

Suddenly, frightened by the sudden violence of the storm, the boys made a dash for Logan's back door. Once inside, the excitement quickened as the television warned of flash flooding.

"Please stay inside," the voice pleaded. "Bridges are washed out, and power and phone lines are already down all over the city." Then the screen went black.

Logan ran to the window only to see the power lines all over the Wesson's backyard, writhing like angry serpents as they emitted smoke and fire. Joey grabbed the phone, but the line was dead.

Papaw, awakened by the thunder from his afternoon nap, came into the room. "Looks like our daily storm, huh, guys?' he said sleepily.

"No, Papaw, it's much worse today. The wind and lightning have knocked out the power and phone lines," said Logan excitedly. " The bridges are out all over town."

Just then there was a knock at the door. It was Mr. Wesson. "I almost didn't make it," he said. "I've never seen it rain so much so quickly. Let's hurry, Joey. Your grandma needs her medication now," he added.

"But, Grandpa, we can't. There's wires all over the yard and the ground is full of electricity," Joey responded.

"We can't even call the Power Company, because the phone is dead," Logan added.

Precious time was lost as they tried to decide on a plan of action. It would take at least an hour of driving out of the way to the Power Company and even then all their crews would probably be out trying to restore power. Logan knew enough about diabetes to understand that Mrs. Wesson could go into a coma before then.

Suddenly, he knew exactly what he had to do. "Papaw, she can give herself the shot. I've seen her do it before. I can take the insulin to her on the high wire."

"I don't know, Logan. It's too dangerous." He loved his grandson too much to put him in harms way.

"I've done it a hundred times. Please, there's no other way," Logan begged.

Mr. Wesson was trying hard not to look worried and Joey was fighting to hold back the tears as Papaw looked into their faces. "We'll probably be in big trouble when your dad finds out, but it seems the only way," he finally conceded.

Thankfully, the storm ended as quickly as it had begun, but it would still be hours before the water receded and the power was restored.

As he tied his shoes and put the bottle of insulin in his pocket, Logan felt excitement mixed with fear he'd never felt before. He climbed the ladder and looked at the rushing water below. The wires still spewed smoke and sparks.

He whispered a prayer. " Dear God, please help me across to Mrs. Wesson before it's too late." He felt an overwhelming sense of calm as he began his trek over the wire. The trip probably lasted no more than ten minutes, but to Logan it seemed like an eternity. He finally was able to bend down and grasp the cable with both hands and swung to the safety of the Wesson's porch and Mrs. Wesson's embrace. Several of the neighbors had witnessed his heroic feat and they gave a loud cheer.

Hours later, the stream now calm and the power restored, Logan was relaxing with his parents and Papaw. His dad answered the door to find a reporter and photographer from the daily newspaper along with an aide from the mayor's office. Joey and his parents and grandparents brought up the rear.

Mrs. Wesson spoke first. "We couldn't wait any longer to honor our hero." She had tears in her eyes.

Joey's dad added. "We brought your birthday present a day early to show our appreciation." With that, he rolled in a new ten speed bike like the one Logan had dreamed about.

This was a night Logan would never forget. The pictures and the interview for the paper were memorable enough, as was the certificate signed by the mayor. But what pleased him most was when Papaw put his arm around him and said, "May I present my grandson, the future doctor, Logan Gamble."

That ended a perfect day.

HOG KILLING TIME

After the first frost, usually in November, it was time to butcher the hogs and get ready for winter. We usually had five or six big ones. The neighbors would all gather early in the morning to help, and the next few days would be spent in returning the favor.

The .22 rifle would be brought out and a decision had to be made. Who was the best shot? This was a critical time since the hog needed to be brought down with the first shot, between the eyes.

Someone would then rush across the hog pen and sever the jugular vein with a big homemade knife. A log chain would be secured around the carcass, which would then be hitched to a mule and dragged unceremoniously across the pen to a vat of scalding water. This consisted of a metal tub placed over a shallow pit filled with burning embers.

The carcass would be submerged in the hot water and everyone, including the children, would gather around to scrape the hair from the hog. The odor from the wet hair seemed unbearable until the hog was hooked to a pulley and hoisted to a sturdy limb of an old post oak tree. Then you realized you didn't know the meaning of bad smell until the belly was ripped open and the entrails spilled out into a number-two wash tub.

When the warm entrails came in contact with the crisp morning air, causing steam to rise from the tub, I always vowed to become a vegetarian. That vow was quickly forgotten for another year the following day when we feasted on fresh sausage for breakfast and tenderloin for the noon meal.

Some people would wash the entrails and eat them as "chitlins". We always dug a deep hole and buried them.

After the insides of the carcass had been thoroughly washed it was removed from the limb of the oak and the task of cutting it up would begin.

Hams and shoulders would be salted down to cure. The shoulders would provide meat for the winter. At our house country hams were a luxury we couldn't afford. My dad would take them to the general store that a distant cousin owned in the county seat and trade them for "due bills" to be used for staple groceries the following year.

As the long day ended and dusk fell Momma would remove the blue checkered oilcloth from the oak table and secure the meat grinder to one side. We would spend the next hours grinding sausage, mixing in just the right amount of sage, pepper, and salt. We would stuff the sausage into bags made from flour sacks.

Long after midnight we would finally get to bed, knowing that in a few hours the process would begin all over again as we returned the favor to a neighbor.

JOSHUA RABBIT MAKES A NEW FRIEND

Joshua Rabbit was enjoying the fine autumn day in the enchanted forest when his mother called to him. "Josh, I want you to take this fresh carrot pie to Mrs. Cottontail. She hasn't been feeling well and maybe this will cheer her up."

Josh didn't want to stop playing in the leaves, but he always obeyed his parents. "Very well, Mother, but may I stop at Ollie Otter's house and show him my new coat you and Father bought me for my birthday?" he asked.

"You may visit for a few minutes, but don't go near the railroad tracks," warned his mother. "The Bobcat family lives just on the other side, and we never associate with those animals."

The sunshine was reflecting off the gold and brown leaves, and dreamy eyed Josh was soon chasing a butterfly. The pie sat forgotten on a stump near the railroad tracks while he had the time of his life.

Suddenly, there was a chill in the air. He realized it was almost sundown and he had left the road and lost the carrot pie.

"I'm lost and it will be getting dark soon," he thought as he frantically searched for the main road. Just then he heard a cry.

"Please, help me! My baby is on the tracks, and my

foot is caught in a vine and the train is due."

Then Josh heard the train whistle and ran up the hill to the tracks. There was Billy Bobcat happily playing with a colony of ants.

Josh thought of all the bad things he had heard about the Bobcat family and started to leave the baby. "Maybe his mother will free herself and get to him in time," he thought wishfully. At that very moment the big train came into sight, and without another thought Josh grabbed the baby Bobcat and rolled off the tracks just as the locomotive went past.

He lost his footing and rolled almost on top of Mrs. Bobcat. Josh had never felt such fear before. He was sure something terrible was going to happen to him. He dropped the baby and ran over the tracks and found his way to the main road. The carrot pie and Ollie Otter were forgotten as he rushed to the safety of his home.

His father was home and dinner was on the table. "Where have you been?" demanded his mother. "I've been worried sick that something had happened to you."

"Mother, Father, I'm sorry, but I lost the pie, and I've gotten my new coat dirty. Please let me tell you what happened," he begged.

When he finished his story, his parents were not sure he was telling the truth. They were about to send him to bed without any dinner when there was a knock at the door. To their surprise there stood the Bobcat family. Mr. Bobcat was holding little Billy, and Mrs. Bobcat had the long-lost carrot pie in her hand.

"Please, don't be frightened," she said softly." I know that ever since the humans built the railroad tracks through the forest the animals on one side have not had anything to do with the ones on the other side. But your son did a very brave thing today, and we had to thank him for it."

Father Rabbit quickly overcame his fear and said, "Please, come in. We didn't believe Joshua, and we owe him an apology."

"I guess we can all learn a lesson from this," said Mr. Bobcat.

"Come," said mother Rabbit, "have some catnip tea. I'm so ashamed of how we've acted these past few years."

Soon the adults were laughing and talking as though they were old friends, while Josh happily rollicked with Billy on the floor.

"We want you to have Sunday dinner with us, and later we'll visit some of our friends to let them get to know you," insisted Father Rabbit.

After the Bobcats had gone home and Josh was getting ready for bed, his parents came into his room.

"We're very proud of what you did today, Josh. Tomorrow you can take the pie to Mrs. Cottontail and spend as much time with Ollie Otter as you wish."

Joshua went to sleep a very happy little rabbit.

Note: This story was written shortly after my first grandchild, Joshua, was born. I hope it will help some youngster to realize we all have prejudices, but with a little understanding of other people's feelings we can overcome those prejudices and live harmoniously with our neighbors.

POKE SALET

My daddy loved poke salet and my momma loved to cook it for him. In the spring when the weather warmed and the ground thawed it wasn't long before the shoots of the pokeweed thrust their heads through the rich West Tennessee soil.

My daddy would pick the young tender leaves and Momma would wash them over and over. Then she would parboil them, warning that poke was poisonous if not parboiled.

She would drain the water from the cooked greens then mix several scrambled eggs with them, add a little salt, and then put them in a hot skillet of bacon grease.

I never liked poke salet as a child, but after I was married I asked my wife to cook some for me. I don't know if I tasted the poke and eggs or if I was relishing a childhood memory. Whatever the case I realized my daddy had gourmet tastes when it came to eating poke salet.

LASSIE

She came to our house in the springtime with another dog who had a broken jaw.

Someone from town decided they no longer needed a couple of mangy dogs.

We never turned away strays, human or animal.

We named the little one with the broken jaw Whitey, for obvious reasons.

But the brownish-gold female earned her name by her actions.

Momma would be taking the laundry down from the clothesline, and the dog would take towels and other pieces in her mouth and bring them inside.

When we took a load of "stove wood" to the kitchen to burn in the range she would pick up a stick and deliver it as well.

Someone in the family had read "Lassie, Come Home." So she became Lassie.

My brother suffered from severe Downs Syndrome, and though he was about eight years old his mind never matured beyond two.

My mother would put a quilt on the front porch and

he would spend the day on this pallet.

Lassie adopted "Baby Ray", a name I gave him when he was born.

As spring plowing began she would sometimes follow my brothers as they tilled the fields.

One day the sharp point of the plow destroyed a rabbit's nest, killing one baby rabbit and leaving two others to die.

Lassie took the dead one in her mouth and brought it home.

She gently laid it on Baby Ray's pallet.

At first we thought she had killed it. After all, that is what dogs do to rabbits.

Then she returned to the field and gently took another in her mouth and repeated her journey.

She made a third trip and brought the other live rabbit to Baby Ray.

We fed them cow's milk from a medicine dropper and they grew and flourished.

They would lay on the pallet and allow Baby Ray to pet them. We named them Dan and Hal, after my brothers' two horses.

Strangely, our other two dogs, Brownie and Rattler, never tried to harm these rabbits.

We tried several times, unsuccessfully, to return the rabbits to the fields after they were grown, but each time they would follow us back home.

We were finally able to lose them in the woods and they never came back.

Late in the afternoon our farm animals, two mules, a horse, and our two milch cows would be on the far side of the pasture at milking time.

My dad would sit on the front porch and tell Lassie to go bring Rosie Lee, our milch cow, to the barn for milking.

I don't know how she understood, but she would race through the pasture, get behind Rosie, and begin barking and nipping at her heels.

Soon she would bring her to the barn, and I would proceed to do the milking. Lassie was Baby Ray's watchdog. No one could get near him if Lassie didn't know the person.

God works in strange ways sometimes, His wonders to perform.

SIXTY SIX YEARS AND COUNTING

Sixty-six years just ended
and the glass is still half full.

Today I begin my sixty-seventh year
on this ball of mud we call earth.

It would be easy to become cynical.

After all, while I slept last night,
more than ten thousand fellow
human beings died of starvation.

The news channels are filled with stories
of political corruption,
and everyone seems to be screaming
for special treatment.

The "it ain't my fault" syndrome seems to be of epidemic proportions in America.As I reflect on the negative things in our society I'm suddenly surrounded and embraced by four pairs of arms and smiling faces. "Happy Birthday, Pawpaw."

The little white fuzz ball we think is a dog licks my face as if to say "me too, me too."

I realize how blessed I am and I thank God for youth and enthusiasm and optimism.

May I always see the glass half full.

LISTEN TO THE HILLS

Take a walk through my forested knolls. Lose yourself among my mighty oaks.

Listen to the fresh water spring as it gurgles from a hillside.

Sh-h-h! Lie down upon a carpet of leaves beneath the shelter of a mighty beech tree.

Listen carefully: I have stories to tell.

It was 1863 and war had come to West Tennessee.

Some of my children wore the Union Blue, while others chose the gray of the Confederacy.

Not more than a mile from here two brothers grew to manhood. They used to hunt here where game was plentiful.

When war came they chose different sides, the older blue and the younger gray.

My son in blue was sent north to Virginia. The one in gray went south to Vicksburg.

I breathed a sigh of relief that they would never face one another in battle.

But fate would not be denied.

As the war progressed they moved from one unit to another.

They found themselves here, not far from their boyhood home.

Forrest's troops faced Ingersoll and his Union band on a sunny Sunday afternoon.

As the battle began the armies raced toward one another. Amid much shooting and other loud noises only a few causalities were suffered on either side.

The brothers rushed forward into the fray, stopping short as they saw one another.

They dropped their weapons and ran across the meadow with outstretched arms.

They were face to face when an artillery shell exploded nearby. They both fell mortally wounded.

The firing stopped on both sides, although neither commander had ordered it.

Silently, men in blue and gray moved slowly toward the still forms.

They lay in a final embrace, much the same as they did as children in a shared bed on a cold winter night.

No officer dared rebuke either side as the war-weary soldiers gently lifted the bodies and buried them beneath the green grass of my meadow.

TURTLEDOVES, DEVIL'S HORSES AND SNAKE DOCTORS

A TRIBUTE TO MOMMA

My mother was a remarkable woman. Although she had very little formal education, she was an extremely intelligent lady.

She was born on a tobacco farm in Trigg County, Kentucky, May 27, 1897. Married at age nineteen, she gave birth to ten children. I was number eight, and she was thirty-eight years old.

She had a very hard life. My dad was a West Tennessee dirt farmer who never owned the land he worked.

She lost her second born son at twenty months old. She preserved a lock of his hair in her Bible. Now, eighty years later, my sister still has it.

My brother, born two years after me when Momma was forty years old, suffered from an extreme case of Downs Syndrome.

The last child, my youngest brother, was born when she was forty-two. His IQ was so high it was off the charts.

They're both deceased.

Momma had a stroke in 1946. I was eleven years old. It was a Saturday in November and the entire family was in the county seat as usual.

My two younger brothers and I were at home with her. She spent the remainder of my childhood trying to overcome the devastating effects of the stroke.

I've often wondered how different my life would have been if she had remained healthy.

Before her stroke I remember many pleasant things about Momma. She never wanted her boys to kill a bird if it wasn't edible. But she strictly prohibited anyone from even thinking about killing a turtledove, her name for the mourning dove.

She would remind us of the part the dove played in the biblical account of Noah's Ark and the Flood. She was convinced that underneath each wing was the letter G for God. To her, the dove was God's bird and off limits to all the hunters in the family.

It was years later that I learned that the breast of the dove was considered a delicacy.

The praying mantis is also known as the walking stick in some parts of the country, but to Momma it was the devil's horse. It is such an ugly insect it wasn't difficult for a small boy to envision a miniature Satan astride its back. I had a fear of the devil's horse for many years until I found out it is quite harmless.

The swampy area around our farm pond was a favorite place for the dragonfly. To Momma it was a "snake doctor." She would warn us children to stay away from the pond if there were "snake doctors" present. She would say that was a sure sign there were snakes nearby.

We lived so far from school that I was seven and my sister almost ten years old before we moved close enough to enroll us. That didn't stop Momma. She would use old textbooks, erasing the answers and drilling us with them.

She taught us to read, write, count, and know the alphabet. Needless to say we were probably far ahead of our peers when we did start school.

The county school superintendent even moved my sister to third grade immediately. I think I got to skip "primer," our name for modern day kindergarten.

We both did extremely well in school, thanks to Momma "home schooling" us before that term had even been invented.

When I was a child there were times when I was embarrassed that she didn't have nice clothes to wear, or that she refused to cut her hair. Now, in retrospect, I see a woman who loved her family and faced life with all its problems with dignity.

I shall never forget Momma.

HOPE

I dreamed again last night,
the dream I had as a child.

The world was bathed in beauty,
and hate never reared its ugly head.
The children played together, of every race and creed.

The parents loved their children above all else.
There was no greed nor selfishness, no

Slaughter of the unborn innocents.

The morning sun streams through my window
and I awaken.

A tear forms in my eye as I realize it was only a
dream. Selfishness and greed are once more in command.

Thousands will die today for lack of food and no
one seems to care.

Outside my window I can hear the voices of children, happily playing together,
and I thank my Creator for hope.

There is always hope.

DAD

"Where you goin', Dad?"

"Gotta go plow the fields today, sonny boy."

"Can I go?"

"No, sonny boy, it's too hot and you're too little."

"But I wanna go with you."

He stoops down and I think I've overdone it.
He's gonna spank me for sure.

But this time he picks me up with his big, callused
hands, like leather from so many years
of labor in the fields.

He hugs me to his chest; my face snuggles
against the stubble of his beard.

I feel his heart beating through the DC overalls bib.

He smells like pipe tobacco and sweat.
Not an odor, just sweat.

He holds me for a few minutes then puts me
down and strides out the door.

I run to the window, tears streaming down my
cheeks.

He takes the harness lines and urges
the team of mules forward.

I watch as he goes past the white clapboard house
where the landlord lives.

He disappears over the hill.

He must be a hundred miles away by now and
it'll be a hundred hours before I see him again.

I press my nose against the window pane,
waiting for the dinner bell to ring telling the
farm hands it's time for a noon break.

I can't wait for Dad to get home.

It was 1939 and I was not yet four years old.

I don't remember Dad ever picking me up
and hugging me again.

It's been more than six decades and I can still
feel the warmth and security I felt
that day so long ago.

I'm in the winter of my life now
and before too many more years I'll come to
the still waters of Jordan.

Jesus will take my hand and gently lead me across.

My Heavenly Father will lift me into his arms
and there I'll rest for eternity.

MY WIFE

We sit quietly in the living room on an early November day. It's Saturday and the housework is done. Now it's time to relax, I with a book and she knitting and watching an old Cary Grant movie.

The afternoon sun streams through the window and casts a ray across her face, and she looks like my bride again.

The movie has brought forth just the hint of tears.

As I steal a look at her during this vulnerable moment I think back over more than three decades and three children ago.

I feel an overpowering sense of guilt for all the times I failed her.

I wasn't always a good husband or father. I've suffered in silent anguish from a guilty conscience.

When the children were small we had one income, one car, and not enough house. There was always too much month left at the end of the money. But she never complained.

She was homemaker, dressmaker, barber, and financial planner.

When I got carried away and tended to float on a cloud, she was the practical one who anchored my feet in reality.

She conquered the heathen, not by preaching, but by her own quiet example of Christ like living. Miracle of miracles, I was eventually baptized.

The greatest tribute any parent can receive is to hear their children speak of a happy childhood. In this, she is a millionaire.

What did I ever do to deserve to be loved by someone like her?

As the calendar announces the approaching winter, we too, are about to enter the winter season of life.

I don't fear the dark clouds of uncertainty as I eagerly anticipate the future.

I have loved and been loved and hand in hand we will walk the corridor of life together.

Would that every man could be as blessed as I. This woman, this beautiful creation of God makes everyday a pleasure.

My strength, my encouragement, the love of my life.

My wife.

A TRIBUTE TO JOSH, LOGAN, KAITLYN, AND MORGAN

MY REASONS FOR LIVING

Dark clouds form on the horizon, thunder rolls across the earth, lightning flashes from every direction, the wind is so strong even the mighty oaks bend before its force.

The day is black as night, there is no movement of animals, the birds stop their singing, the flowers wilt and their petals fall to the ground, there is sadness in the world.

Suddenly, the storm ceases, the lightning stops, the thunder loses its power, and the black clouds give way to the golden circle of sun against an azure blue sky.

I am lifted up and seated on a golden throne and a diamond-studded crown is placed on my head. I hear voices of angels singing, and in the distance are the strings of a thousand violins, playing Mozart, Bach, Tchaikovsky and Strauss.

The sky is filled with the beauty of every describable bird. The flowers re-gain their own beauty magnified a thousand times over. I am a happy man and life is good.

This is what happens when you enter the room and put your arms around me and say, "I LOVE YOU, PAW-PAW."

My Grandchildren
My Reasons For Living

SKINNY DIPPING IN COTTONMOUTH CREEK

Summers are hot in West Tennessee, and 1947 was no exception. School was out to allow the kids to help chop cotton. It was Saturday afternoon in late June, and four unlikely fourteen-year-olds were engaging in their favorite pastime.

"Ah-h-h, the water feels great." Mel Briscoe eased his thin body down on the damp bank and dangled his feet in the slow-moving creek. A few yards downstream, Cottonmouth Creek widened into what had become the swimming hole.

Butch Avery was strutting his perfect build in front of the Smith twins before leaping into the water. "Melvin's a sissy," he taunted as he leaped into the water.

Mel, red-faced, weakly replied, "You know I'm allergic to the cottonwood fuzz. I'll break out if I take my clothes off."

Billy Smith defended Mel. "Aw, c'mon Butch, you know he can't swim."

"Yeah, lay off, Butch. Mel's an all right guy," added R.L., the other twin.

"Oh, go whittle on a stick, Melvin," Butch retorted as

he splashed noisily in the creek.

"Maybe he'll lay off me for awhile," Melvin hoped. He started to work on a hickory limb with his Swiss army knife. He thought he'd make a slingshot stock for his little brother.

Downstream the Smith twins were competing as usual. "Beat ya to the other side," Billy challenged his brother. "That'll be the day," said R.L., accepting the dare. They made it across the widest part of the creek, touching the bank at the same time.

"Tied again, huh?" said Mel, laughing.

The leaves barely moved on the large cottonwoods along the creek bank. The afternoon air was hot and stifling. Mel watched as the sun wove its patterns of liquid gold on the water's surface. He loved it here. It was worth the ribbing he took from Butch just to listen to the sounds of nature. "I wish I was more like Butch," he thought wistfully. "Everything seem to come so easy for him."

Butch had climbed onto the "grown-up" diving board and was about to do a backward flip as Billy tried to stop him. Mel yelled, "Butch, don't try that! Remember what happened to the guy from town last year. He broke his neck!"

"The water's not deep enough, Butch," added R.L.

"Oh, all right. You're all a bunch of old ladies," Butch protested. He reluctantly climbed down and jumped into the water from the bank.

The long afternoon dragged on. The unlikely group of friends continued to enjoy it, each boy in his separate way. Mel was putting the final touches on his masterpiece. The twins were having a water fight for the tenth time. High in a tree a blue jay was fussing at a nearby squirrel.

Suddenly, Butch let out a bloodcurdling scream. "Snake!" he cried. The twins scrambled up the muddy bank, grabbing their jeans.

Butch leaped from the water with the biggest cottonmouth water moccasin Mel had ever seen hanging from his ankle. Legs flailing in the air, Butch managed to shake it loose. It flew through the air, its mouth open. The inside looked just like a boll of cotton. The snake hit the water with a sickening thud and quickly disappeared under the roots of the overhanging trees

"I'm gonna die, I'm gonna die!" wailed Butch. The twins, not knowing what to do, were scrambling to get into their jeans. They were at least a half-mile from the nearest house, and none of them had ever seen a snakebite before.

Mel was paralyzed with fear, but as Butch continued to moan and scream, he remembered that last school year the nurse had shown them how to make an incision and suck the poison from the wound. A sudden change came over him as he realized he was Butch's only hope.

Wiping the blade of his knife on his jeans he said, "Lay on your stomach, Butch. Billy, make a tourniquet out of your T-shirt and tie it below his knee.

"R.L., run and get your daddy and his pick-up. We've got to get him to a doctor, " he ordered.

Stunned by the sudden change in their shy friend, they responded. It seemed almost like a dream to Mel as he instructed Billy to hold Butch's leg. He made quarter-inch incisions directly on the fang punctures.

"Hold him still, Billy," he said as he put his mouth over the cuts and sucked out the bloody poison. He spat out a mouthful and Butch, seeing the blood, fainted. Mel continued to suck the venom and blood from the wound. After a few minutes he told Billy to loosen the tourniquet, as Mrs. Horton had showed them last spring.

It seemed like hours before he finally heard the roar of the Smith's old pick-up. Walt Smith came crashing through the underbrush. He scooped Butch up in his massive arms.

"Doc Brandon is waiting for us at the clinic."

He put Butch in the bed of the truck and covered him with a blanket. Mel and the twins loaded in with Butch, who was beginning to come around.

"Man, I'm sick to my stomach," he complained.

Billy, still finding it hard to believe, said, "Butch, Mel sucked out the poison. I bet he saved your life!"

Butch looked at Mel with a new respect "Thanks, man. I owe you one."

Mel, red-faced and once more shy, was embarrassed. "Aw, I didn't do much, just what Mrs. Horton showed us last year."

"Well, I'm sure glad you were paying attention in her class," said Butch.

The truck came to an abrupt halt in front of the clinic and Walt Smith carried Butch inside.

"Lay him on the table, Walt. I've got a new serum that works miracles on snakebites," said Doc Brandon. He was holding a needle that looked a foot long. Butch took one look and fainted again.

Doc injected the serum just above the bite. "I'll call his folks and tell them what happened. They'll need to keep him off that leg for a few days. He'll be good as new in time for school."

The next day, after church, Mel was finishing his second piece of cherry pie when his mother, smiling proudly, said, "You should really go check on Butch. After all, you did save his life."

Mel didn't want to go. "He'll probably find some way to put me down for what I did," he thought. But his mother prevailed, and he walked the short distance to the Averys' farm. Butch was sitting on the front porch with his leg elevated, drinking lemonade.

"Want some?" he offered.

"No, thanks. I was just wondering how you're doin'?"

"I'm fine, thanks to you."

They were both uncomfortable. After staring at the clouds, then the porch, Butch finally spoke "Mel, I've always wanted to play chess, but I never knew anyone but you who played." He fumbled for words. "I was wondering if… if maybe you'd show me?"

Mel couldn't believe his ears. "Sure. How about today? I'll go get my set."

Butch, still having trouble making the words come out, said, "Maybe when we get to high school next week, we could take some classes together, maybe be best friends."Mel, still having a problem taking all this in, put out his hand. "I'd really like that, Butch."

He headed home to get his chess set. "Butch Avery playing chess." he grinned, "The Smith twins'll never believe this." Suddenly, he began to run. Life had never been sweeter.

"Look out high school, here we come."

LEGEND OF THE PECAN TREE

Your large, green boughs, weighted by your fruit, bend downward. You beckon to me as the southern breeze gently caresses you.

You have a story to tell, and I have been chosen to hear your secret. The young soldier is only sixteen, a proud hero returning home.

He had left New Orleans a month before with his pockets filled with pecans. A shortage of rations had caused him to eat most of them on the way.

He had one left, and he was determined to save it for Momma. She'd never seen such a thing.

After a supper of dried beef and biscuit he has joined the others to celebrate.

Soon they will be home. "Let's drink to our victory, and how brave we were."

He stumbles to his tent. This is a new feeling. He has never drunk before.He feels strong and invincible. He can do anything he wants. He is a hero.

It is so dark, and he is trying to keep his balance, when he comes face to face with his sergeant.

"Your quarters are a mess, boy, and you're drunk." He slaps the boy's face. "Pick up the crumbs in front of your tent before you go to bed," he orders.

"I'm a soldier. I'm a hero. I don't have to pick up crumbs. The officers never pick up theirs."

He feels the fire in his gut and the false courage that's found foolishly in a bottle.

Daybreak comes and he's hauled before the brigade commander himself. He's sorry, but there is no forgiveness. Discipline must be maintained. Disobeying a non-commissioned officer is serious.

The colonel walks away for a moment, then suddenly turns and orders, "Death by firing squad.

"Even the sergeant is shocked but knows better than to question the decision.

A firing squad is formed, and the boy's tear-stained cheeks are covered with a dirty rag over his eyes. He begs for the chance to see his mother once more.

The colonel gives the order to carry on and returns to his tent. Three shots break the stillness of the morning. The boy is dead.

A shallow grave is dug on a small bluff overlooking a fresh water spring, and he's buried in his clothes. Only his shoes are removed. Another soldier will benefit from his death.

Long after the army has moved on the body lies in the grave, and the clothes rot away, and the pecan in his pocket sprouts and takes root.

It stands the test of time, and now it's 1945 and I hear his voice in the wind calling for his mother. Sometimes I catch a fleeting glance of him as he moves about behind the giant tree. Then he's gone.

One day I'm alone at home with my mother, and I visit the pecan tree. The sun is warm, and I have an eerie feeling that I'm being watched.

I hear the wind move through the thick branches, and I see a figure emerge from behind the tree. I'm mesmerized by what is happening. Before I think about being scared he cries, "Go home. Your mother needs you. Go home now." Then he disappears as quickly as he had materialized.

I rush home to find my mother on the floor. She tries to get up but she can't. She tries to speak, but her tongue doesn't work.

She has suffered a massive stroke and we're home alone, miles from a doctor. I run to the neighbor's house, and she gets word to my dad and a doctor.

My mother lives, and I go back to the pecan tree to try and figure out what happened.

The breeze is moving through the branches. I hear laughter, and he appears in front of me.

He smiles and says, "Go home to your mother. I'm going home to mine."

The wind never sounded the same after that, but I love to come to this place and think about the young soldier, and imagine him at home with his mother, at last.

One of the oldest and biggest pecan trees in America.
Natchez Trace state Park, Wildersville, Tn

THE DAY THE LADY CRIED

On that fateful Tuesday morning,
as the smoke rose to the sky.

Lady Liberty seemed to bow her head,
a teardrop in her eye.

Who could have imagined that
so many would have died.

For those who looked at her
that day swore The Lady cried.

She has stood with torch uplifted
for five score years and more.

As the huddled mass of people
have disembarked upon her shore.

"Give me your tired, your poor,"
she's begged for, lo, these many years.

With open arms she welcomed them,
to rest from all their cares.

We have come from every corner of earth
to this great land.

Seeking peace and opportunity
and together we will stand.

We all love America,
on this you can depend.

When those who hate attack us,
we're ready to defend.

Our features may not be the same,
with different colored skin.

But our diversity is a sign of strength.
Together we will win.

Those who would attack us and try to bring us down
fail to understand us or where our strength is found.

Our heroes came forward that day,
too numerous to name.

Ordinary people, just regular folks,
who'll now go down in fame.

From a field in Pennsylvania
to New York City and D.C.

Their feats of courage are held up
high for all the world to see.

The smoke still rises to the sky,
as the work below goes on.

Millions of prayers are said each day,
for families now alone.

Those who did these awful things
can try to run and hide.

But we the people shall never forget
the day The Lady cried.

REMEMBERING UNITY SCHOOL

Dedicated to "Miss Elizabeth" Anderson

Saturday, October 6, 2001, was a beautiful autumn day in west Tennessee. The leaves were just beginning to turn and the sky was so blue it literally hurt your eyes to look at it.

Several people met at the Poplar Springs Baptist church for a reunion of former students who had attended the small community schools before the county system was consolidated in the early fifties. Some of us had not seen one another for more than fifty years. Though our bodies showed the ravages of time, with wrinkles and excess body weight, I think everyone would agree we shared a spirit of love and friendship than transcends time and physical change.

Miss Avel Grissom, who taught many of us, had put this together for the past three years, but this was my first time to attend. Lord willing it would not be my last.

There were many schools represented, but I want to put my emphasis on Unity where I spent all my elementary school years.

I was born July 21, 1935 on the Jim Milam farm not more than a few hundred yards from the school building. New Unity was the third in succession of school buildings and had been built the year before. By the time I was school age we had moved across the creek to the Albert Fesmire place and it was too far to walk to school. Fortunately for my sister Elsie Dean (Deanie) and me, our mother took the time to teach us to read, write, count, and say the alphabet. When Deanie was almost ten and I was seven we moved again to the Ernest Threadgill place within a mile of school, so we were finally enrolled.

We were put in primer, which I suppose was the forerunner of kindergarten. Miss Willie D. Parham was the teacher for the lower grades. My sister was so far advanced Miss Willie D. put her up to the blackboard with some of the students from higher grades, and she bested the lot of them. Mr. Granville Bartholomew, the principal and fifth through eighth grade teacher, was called to witness her performance. He notified Mr. Ira C. Powers, the county school superintendent, and after they conferred they agreed she should be moved immediately to the third grade.

I remember when we had spelling bees she and I would be left standing after everybody else was seated. I would like to say I then beat her, but that wouldn't be true.

The Britt family was poor among a community of poor people; we were so poor we made the others look middle class.

We had some good teachers at Unity, but some were better than others. I remember "Miss Jessie" Fisher. I'm sure she loved us, but she never had children of her own, and, perhaps unknowingly, she made me feel inferior and not of much value. I loved to read and that was ultimately my salvation. I learned if I could read well I could educate myself, and years later I set about to do that very thing.

Our library at Unity consisted of a bookcase in each room filled with the most delightful books. It wasn't long before I had read all the ones in Miss Willie D's room, and when the others would go outside for recess I would sneak into Miss Jessie's room and read the books designed for the older kids. One in particular sticks in my mind even today, fifty-five years later. It was *The Seven Wonders of the World*, written by Richard Haliburton, who, I was to learn much later, had been born in Brownsville, Tennessee, and raised in Memphis. He was an adventurer and lost his life somewhere in the Pacific during World War Two. No one knows how for sure. I could literally lose myself in his book and escape my dreary world for at least a few minutes. Miss Jessie would find me reading and make me go outside and play.

I remember she gave me the only whipping I received in all my school years. I was walking home with my brother's stepson, Junior Brewer, and Billie Hayes and Cornelia Hamlet when he began to pick on them. I saw myself as their Knight in shining armor and decided to put a stop to his pranks. As usual, a fight ensued.

Unfortunately, Miss Jessie was heading home in her 1939 Chevrolet and looked across the field and witnessed our scuffle. The following morning she whipped both of us with a twelve-inch ruler. That didn't hurt, but when I got home my dad used a peach tree switch on my legs, and I remembered that for a long time!

The two teachers who most impacted my life were Avel Grissom and Lunelle Shelby. They both seemed to understand that in order to teach you must first convince the student that he can learn. I can never repay them for making me feel like I was somebody.

I remember the "stews" we had to raise funds for the PTA. I'm certain we got an extra measure of protein in every bowl with the addition of numerous grasshoppers and other insects. It was probably flavored, too, with tobacco juice, since many of the men charged with the task of stirring the stew to keep it from burning were avid snuff dippers or tobacco chewers. I wonder what the Health Department would say about that today? It didn't make anyone sick though.

I remember Miss Elizabeth and Bill Anderson were always there to support the school, along with Mrs. Bess Russell and Mrs. Dora Whittle. I'm sure there were many more, but these folks stick out in my memory.

I would be remiss if I failed to give credit to "Miss" Lola Milam who only had a third grade education but was our substitute teacher on many occasions. Oh, would that our degreed teachers today in public schools were as qualified to mold young minds as these true servants were.

Across the road and next to the building was the Milam property known, for obvious reasons, as the "flatwoods." The Milams would not permit any hunting, so consequently there was an assortment of wildlife on the premises. Anyone caught there with a gun faced the wrath of Miss Lola's shotgun. The tall oak trees were covered with muscadine vines as thick as a man's arm, and these, too, were off limits. However, it seems I managed to enjoy the black, succulent fruit on many a fall day.

The physical building was not impressive. It consisted of two large rooms divided by two blackboards, which could be raised when we put on a school play on the stage of the "big kids" room. There was a small porch where I remember leaving my mud caked four buckle overshoes (when we could afford them). I also remember standing, head bowed, while someone was praying inside and we were running late.

There was a "side room" tacked onto the back and opening into the principal's room. In my early years we carried our lunch in a paper bag or a lard bucket with holes punched in the lid to keep the inside from "sweating." Many days the Britt kids' lunch was a biscuit with a fried egg in between. When we didn't have fried pies Momma would fill a pie shell with butter and sugar and fry those for our dessert. More than once some kid who could afford a store bought lunch would trade with us for our "sugar pies".

When we finally got hot lunches Mrs. Ed Wilson became our cook, and could she ever cook! We would go outside and line up, then troop though the tiny kitchen, fill our plates, and go to our desks to eat. I had never eaten spinach before. I acquired a taste for it then, and to this day it is one of my favorite vegetables.

There was an icehouse just outside the kitchen door with thick walls insulated with sawdust. I believe Bill Anderson and some other dads built it. Out by the softball field was a hand pump and further out, much further, was the girls' toilet. Across the ball field was the boys.

Two other events stand out in my mind, the first being the ice cream supper or box supper, both fundraisers for the PTA. In my memories at least, that homemade ice cream seemed to taste so much better than it does today. That's the wonderful thing about our memory: it filters out all unpleasantness and leaves the good stuff.

The other thing I remember was the movies, which came much later. A Mr. And Mrs. Martin, I think, would come up from Jackson every Wednesday night and show a full length film along with cartoons and the ever-popular serial movie, which would continue for weeks. I still remember scaring the other kids on the way home with my "Wolfman" face and cries. I thought I was a better Wolfman than the star, Lon Chaney Jr.

There was one more teacher that I remember, though vaguely. His name was Travis McMinn. He was only nineteen years old and had spent a few months in the Navy Reserve. I can't remember why he was there as principal (he wasn't even a good teacher,) but I believe he must have filled in for less than a full year. I remember how he would spend recess playing with the bigger boys. Once he tied Joe Russell to a tree and left him while we went back to class. He was also the first person I ever saw who would catch a snake and allow it to wrap around his arm.

I had a boss once who told me I could learn as much from a bad manager as I could from a good one. I would know what to do to avoid being a bad manager, as well. I think, perhaps, this describes my feelings about Travis McMinn.

I have enjoyed this little jaunt down memory lane and I hope anyone who takes the time to read it will enjoy it, as well. My hope is that the community could purchase the old building and restore it and put it to good use as a community center and museum.

REMEMBRANCES

Memories, filtered by the passing of time, none of the bad remembered, only the good.

First date, nervous and unsure, first kiss, terrified, puppy loves left behind in our childhood.

A young soldier away from home, across the mighty Atlantic, homesick, listening to strains of Tchaikovsky waft across the beach on the blue Mediterranean.

Thinning hair turning gray, muscles turning to flab, can't remember what happened yesterday, but memories from the past become clearer and more vivid with each passing day.

Filtered by the sands of time, only the good remains.

AN UNSPOKEN SERMON

In 1940 I was five years old and my family consisted of Dad, Momma, and nine kids. One had died as an infant. My dad was farming someone else's land, as he did all his life. Times were hard — the Depression was still casting a long shadow over Henderson County, Tennessee.

Our closest neighbors, after the landlord, were Joe and Ella Yarbrough and their grandson, Joe L. They were black, or as was considered socially acceptable at the time, "colored." Joe farmed someone else's land, too. He also barbecued a hog once in awhile and sold it to the neighbors to help put food on the table. Joe Yarbrough knew how to barbecue. He was also known to make a little "moonshine" and sell it to the "white folks." He enjoyed a good reputation in that endeavor as well.

My earliest memories of the Yarbroughs were when they would come over in late fall to help kill hogs. Then from time to time Momma would be too sick to wash the clothes, and she would pay Ella to do it for her. I remember calling her "Miss Ella," even though a white male child was never expected to show that sort of respect for black women.

One Christmas I got a red wagon from Santa Claus. I have no idea where my folks found the money for it. I can remember pulling Joe L., who was a bit older than me, in the wagon; then he'd pull me. It never occurred to either of us that we were doing something that some would find unacceptable.

After crops were "laid by" in the fall Dad and Joe would cut logs for cross ties for the railroad to supplement the little return on their crops. I distinctly remember something that happened one day when they came home to eat dinner — which is what we called the noon meal in the country. Joe stood in the kitchen, cap in hand and said to Momma, " Miz Britt, if you'll give me my plate I'll go eat on the back porch."

My dad said, "No, we've worked together all morning. You'll eat at the table with me." Momma had already fed us kids, and I still have a mental picture of my dad sitting across the large homemade table from Joe as they both ate their lunch.

My dad had a brother and a brother-in-law who were Baptist ministers, and we never missed the Holiness Church revival, though I cannot remember a single sermon I ever heard when I was a child. But I have never forgotten the "sermon" my parents preached to me that day.

Several years later when I moved to Jackson I learned two things. Whites and blacks didn't socialize and the Republican Party was made up of rich people. Now the secret was finally out. No wonder I got a red wagon for Christmas. My family was rich and they never told me.

WE ARE HIS CHILDREN

We were like children, lost in the night,

Begging for someone to show us the light.

But when we found Jesus, our faith became sight.

We're no longer in darkness; we're children of light.

CHORUS

We are God's children. Our faith makes us whole.

We are God's children. Christ's blood makes us bold.

His death on the cross has ransomed our soul.

Now, we are God's children, secure in his fold.

In sin we were sinking to depths of despair,
Our souls slowly dying, with no one to care.
God's love overwhelmed us with mercy to spare.
Now we have Jesus, our burdens to bear.

REPEAT CHORUS

Do you know a sinner in darkness today
Who's looking for someone to show them the way?
Tell them about Jesus, please don't delay.
We're children of light, if His words we obey.

REPEAT CHORUS

SPRINGTIME

The north wind still has a chill in it. Winter trying desperately to hold on.

The smell of burning leaves and fresh turned earth herald the coming of spring.

A spring shower comes quickly and washes away the last bit of snow and ice still clinging to the tree roots.

Just as quickly, it stops raining and the clouds give way to the yellow ball of sun against an azure blue sky.

The rich soil yields a treasure for the robins as they enjoy the feast of red worms exposed by the plow.

After the planting comes the summer, then the autumn harvest follows.

The farmers take the bounty from the earth that the Creator has provided.

Like the robins of spring they now enjoy the gifts of a loving God.

Life is good.

LOVE AND FORGIVENESS

When we hurt, hate comes easy. Strike back, get revenge, give us our pound of flesh.

When we hurt, forgiveness comes hard. How can we forgive such a dastardly act?

September 11, 2001, brought all these feelings and emotions to the forefront.

Satan entered the hearts and minds of mankind in the garden.

God saw His beloved children turn away from the blessings He had prepared for us.

Only by allowing that which was His most treasured possession, His Son, to live among us and die for us could He ever hope to bring us home again.

Forgiveness is hard to give when we look at the carnage caused by a few madmen.

But almost two thousand years ago He showed us how.

Forgive them, Father, they know not what they do."

God bless America, and all her hurting children.

WEST TENNESSEE SUMMER

Hot and sticky, humidity in the eighties,

Still not raining…

Lightin' bugs so thick you can read a

Newspaper by them…

A quarter moon tilted upward in the eastern sky,

Promising rain...

Churning buttermilk on the front porch

While swatting flies...

The screech of tree frogs vying for attention

Over the crickets. . .

Dust swirling up in the path of the only car

To pass this way all day...

Filling the cedar bucket with cold water

Drawn from the bowels of the earth...

Scratching chigger bumps in private places,

Knowing Momma is going for the coal oil...

Listening to a soft southern breeze as it

Flirts with the willow tree...

Bathing in a number two wash tub in water

Warmed by the afternoon sun...

Listening to the mournful wails of Mr. Charlie's banjo

As he remembers his old Virginia home...

Watching for the dust cloud up the road

Heralding the iceman's visit...

Playing marbles in the dusty yard while the hens

Scratch for food nearby....

Finding a six foot chicken snake in the hen house,

Lumpy with eggs...

Watching Momma stir the clothes with a broomstick

In the old black wash kettle...

Family time together as we all shuck corn

And break beans on the front porch...

Listening to Dad play "A Wildwood Rose"

On a beat up guitar...

Waiting for Saturday night to turn the battery-

Powered radio to the Grand Ol' Opry…

Whirlwinds, like embryonic tornadoes,

Dancing a ballet in the dust...

Lying on my back under the ancient cedars,

Listening to voices from the past...

Daydreaming on a lazy Sunday afternoon

About faraway places...

Feasting on the black sweet muscadines

On a late summer day...

Memories stream from the past

Like paper from a ticker tape machine...

REMEMBER ME

When the early morning sun glistens like a diamond
from a dew covered rose,

Remember me...

When the thunder crashes and lightning streaks
across the summer sky,

Remember me...

When the first frost of autumn paints nature with its
brush of many colors,

Remember me...

When the silent snow covers all of God's creation in
a blanket of white,

Remember me...

I will be present in the placid face of my devoted
life-mate as she carries on

With life.

I can be seen in the happy smiling faces of my
beloved grandchildren as they look to the future with
a mixture of excitement and anxiety.

When life becomes confusing and filled with uncertainty, remember that a loving Creator watches over
you . . . And remember me

Myrlen Britt is a very "young at heart" sixty-six year old. He happily shares his life with his wife Faye, and their children: one son, two daughters, four grandchildren and a Westie named Buddy.

Myrlen served in the U.S. Army and was honorably discharged with the rank of Sergeant. He is also retired from retail management and ownership. Myrlen has been a member of the church of Christ for much of his life.

His aspirations are to someday take long walks in the park with his *great-grandchildren*, and to author a great novel.